“… h… mov… clad in b… black T-shirt. “What are you doing here?”

He stepped fully into the light, moving lithely, cat-like, toward her, until he was so close she could see the ominous glitter in his beautiful blue eyes. A shiver went down her spine. *She was in trouble. So much trouble.*

His gaze locked onto hers. “When were you going to tell me, Diana? How long did you deem it acceptable to keep from me that I’m going to be a father?”

Her heart leapt into her mouth. *He knew.*

The Tenacious Tycoons

Two billionaire brothers to be reckoned with!

Brothers Harrison and Coburn,
heirs to the great American Grant dynasty,
have everything they could desire—the money,
the power and the tenacity to take whatever they want.
Yet money can't buy everything, and if these brothers
hope to live up to their family legacy they'll each
need a very special woman by their side.

But the rules of love are nothing like those of business—
and when it comes to the game of passion, securing
the deal is never as easy as it first seems…

Read Harrison's story in
Tempted by Her Billionaire Boss
June 2015

And read Coburn's story,
Reunited for the Billionaire's Legacy
October 2015

REUNITED FOR THE BILLIONAIRE'S LEGACY

BY

JENNIFER HAYWARD

Published in Great Britain 2015
by Mills & Boon, an imprint of Harlequin (UK) Limited,
Eton House, 18-24 Paradise Road, Richmond, Surrey, TW9 1SR

ISBN: 978-0-263-24919-4

Harlequin (UK) Limited's policy is to use papers that are natural, renewable and recyclable products and made from wood grown in sustainable forests. The logging and manufacturing processes conform to the legal environmental regulations of the country of origin.

Printed and bound in Spain
by CPI, Barcelona

Jennifer Hayward has been a fan of romance since filching her sister's novels to escape her teenage angst. Her career in journalism and PR—including years of working alongside powerful, charismatic CEOs and travelling the world—has provided her with perfect fodder for the fast-paced, sexy stories she likes to write—always with a touch of humour. A native of Canada's east coast, Jennifer lives in Toronto with her Viking husband and young Viking-in-training.

Books by Jennifer Hayward

Mills & Boon Modern Romance

The Magnate's Manifesto
Changing Constantinou's Game

The Tenacious Tycoons

Tempted by Her Billionaire Boss

Society Weddings

The Italian's Deal for I Do

The Delicious De Campos

The Divorce Party
An Exquisite Challenge
The Truth About De Campo

Visit the Author Profile page at millsandboon.co.uk for more titles.

For my father, a brilliant orthopaedic surgeon, who inspired me to write Diana. You are a real-life hero who has taught me to always aspire to be the best I can be. I will carry that with me always.

And for Rob—thank you for lending your sailing expertise to this story. Much appreciated!

CHAPTER ONE

FOR A MAN who thought life was wrapped in a sea of irony, *this* had to take the cake.

Coburn Grant, heir to an automotive fortune and the newly minted CEO of Grant Industries, gave his silk tie a tug so it didn't feel as if he was choking on his own cynicism. Attending his best friend Tony's engagement party on the eve of his own divorce was impeccable timing that only he could manage. Having to give a speech to the happy couple in thirty minutes that spoke of hope and rainbows? The icing on that exceedingly unpalatable cake.

He could do this. He could. He just needed one more stiff Scotch in his hand. That and a big set of rose-colored glasses.

"You okay, Grant?" Rory Delaney, the big, brawny Australian who had been a close friend since they'd attended Yale together, lifted an amused brow. "You look a bit green."

Coburn adopted one of his patented entertained-by-life expressions, the only mask he ever let the world see. "Never better."

And why wouldn't he be? He was the leader of the Fortune 500 company he'd helped rebuild after his father's death, his brother, Harrison, was campaigning for the White House, which was only adding to Grant Industries' global appeal, and he had a particularly beautiful, slightly wild blonde warming his bed every night—convenient when she lived only two doors down.

Heaven was what he called it.

Rory, a tall, handsome pro basketball player who was immensely popular with the ladies himself, gave a reassured shake of his head. "So glad to hear that, Grant. Right at this particular moment, in fact."

Rory's tone was a blend of sarcasm and warning. He was worrying Coburn was still hung up over his soon-to-be ex, who had left him a year ago. Which was so entirely wrong. His marriage to Diana had been a foolish, rash endeavor to numb the pain he'd been in over his father's death, a passionate, all-consuming obsession with which to direct his emotions. Exactly what he'd needed at the time. Exactly what he needed to get rid of now.

He lifted a shoulder. "I'm not twenty-five anymore, Ror. An amazing body and a smart mouth don't do it for me any longer."

Rory's face tightened in warning as his friend's definitive elocution carried throughout the room. "Coburn—"

He waved him off. "I don't know what you're getting yourself so worked up about. I've got this speech in my back pocket."

Rory gave a spot behind him a pointed look. "Diana is behind you. Three o'clock."

He felt the color drain from his face. "My soon-to-be *ex-wife* Diana?"

"Bingo."

His heart stuttered in his chest, his fingers gripping tighter around the tumbler of whiskey. He'd been ready for this confrontation to happen tomorrow when they had the divorce papers in front of them. When he was prepared to see the woman who had walked out on him without a backward glance twelve months ago, not to be seen since because she'd ensured their schedules never overlapped.

Which wasn't a mean feat in a city like Manhattan, where social circles tended to remain with like social circles.

But then again, Diana didn't socialize. She worked *all the time*. Which made it all the more surprising she was here tonight…

Rage surged through him, swift and all encompassing. It moved upward, through his chest, erupting into his brain to turn it a hazy gray until he thought his head might blow off his shoulders. *How dare she show up here?* How dare she spoil this night for him? These were his friends, not hers.

He drew in a breath through his nose, exhaling slowly as Rory watched him as if he was an overly antagonized bull ready to charge. His turn when he moved was unhurried and deliberate. *Unfazed.* The stricken ebony eyes that stared back at him revealed she'd heard what he'd said. His gaze moved past his outrageously beautiful wife to the group of people standing beside her. They'd *all* heard what he'd said. Well, too bad. He wasn't taking the words back. He'd meant them from the bottom of his heart.

The only thing he *did* regret was showing his hand like that. He'd intended on approaching tomorrow with a calm detachment Diana would have found unnerving. To demonstrate the man she was now dealing with wasn't anything like the one she'd married. That he wasn't a fool for her anymore.

He shifted his attention back to his wife. Her eyes had lost that vulnerable edge now, hardening into the dark, bottomless pools it had once been his life's mission to get to the bottom of. He never had. She was angry. Furious. Too bloody bad. It had been her decision to come.

The entire party was staring at them now, waiting for a reaction from one of them. Mouth tightening, he turned his back on them, but not before cataloging the fact that his soon-to-be ex was even more strikingly beautiful than he remembered her to be. As if life away from him had enhanced her devastating appeal.

He set his glass down on a table, cocked his head toward the bar and he and Rory headed for liquid sustenance. Diana had taken so much from him. But she wasn't ruining tonight.

Not happening.

Diana wobbled in her high-heeled shoes as Coburn shut her out as easily as if she was one of his big-breasted floozies he was long done with. Except he would have been more charming with them. He'd always saved his tough love for her.

Love. An aching knot formed in her throat. The emotion burning in his striking blue eyes just now had been crystal clear. He hated her for what she'd done to him. Still hated her. She wanted to say she hated him back, but that would have been a lie. Her feelings for Coburn had always been far more complex than that. Which was exactly why she needed him to sign the divorce papers tomorrow so she could get on that plane to Africa and forget their marriage had ever existed.

Her hand shook slightly as she averted her gaze from the crowd and lifted her wineglass to her mouth. She knew Coburn had been talking about her. Everyone at the party knew he'd been talking about her. They'd been eating it up like vultures, waiting for the drama to ensue. It was why she hated these damn affairs so much. People with too much time on their hands to speculate and provide yet more salacious tidbits to the gossip mill tomorrow. She'd come only because Annabelle had begged her to.

An amazing body and a smart mouth don't do it for me any longer...

Coburn's words reverberated in her head. She bit back the tremble that wobbled her lower lip and took a sip of the wine. What a bastard he was. She wanted to walk over there and slap his face with the anger that had been festering for twelve months. But that would be letting him win.

She was a surgeon—she put people back together. She would not let Coburn pull her apart. *Again.* Ever.

She made an attempt to circulate, to say polite things to people she hadn't seen in a while and really didn't care to now, but when Coburn was in a room, he was impossible to ignore. He was too beautiful in the male definition of the term. Too tall, with muscles honed by his predilection for daredevil sports, too stunning with his dark hair and arresting blue eyes and too charismatic, with that wicked, effortless charm a woman didn't stand a chance against.

She removed her gaze from the muscles rippling under his shirt, his jacket long ago discarded per usual. Her husband wasn't even that aware of his physical perfection. He traded on his charm, on his ability to get people to do the things he wanted them to do—to make them *beg* to do the things he wanted them to do, without even knowing they were doing it.

Her mouth twisted. She'd never really stood a chance. Her time spent with her nose buried in medical school textbooks, then sequestered in the hospital as a young resident working 24/7 had meant zero time for relationships. When Coburn had swept her off her feet on a rare night out at another Chelsea party very much like this one, he'd just *taken.*

How many people had told her to watch her heart? To use her head. She hadn't listened to any of them. She'd married him despite her father's advice to the contrary.

A dull ache throbbed inside her. She shouldn't have come. She really shouldn't have. She comforted herself knowing soon none of it would matter. Soon she would be on that plane to another continent. She would escape her claustrophobic life with her claustrophobic parents and her claustrophobic job, which was more politics than the Hippocratic oath she'd taken to heal the sick. The suffocating feeling she got every time she remembered Coburn was still sharing this city with her…

Her mouth twisted. If she thought she might be slightly crazy giving up her job at one of New York's most prestigious hospitals to go work in a war-torn territory where the only certainty was complete uncertainty, she wasn't alone. She'd been getting that sentiment a lot lately, particularly from her father, who'd forbidden her to go.

Her gaze drifted to her husband instead of focusing on the conversation happening in the group she'd joined. It hadn't always been bad between her and Coburn. One particular night stuck in her head, in the early days of their marriage. She'd been a rising star as a resident, demonstrating surgical skills way beyond her years. But that night, she'd lost her first patient, a sixteen-year-old boy who'd been in a horrific car accident. His parents had sat in the waiting room for almost eight hours as she and the other specialists had attempted to save him, but the hemorrhaging from his internal injuries had eventually defeated them. She'd arrived home at 7:00 a.m. bruised and battered, her face telling the whole story. Coburn had held her in his arms and rocked her until she'd fallen asleep, then put her to bed. He'd been late for his board meeting that morning, but he hadn't cared. *Then*, they had been the most important thing in each other's orbit.

Her eyes burned at the memory. When they had been good, they had been very, very good. And when they had been bad, it had been unbearable.

Coburn raked a scathing gaze over her from where he stood, talking to Rory. She squared her shoulders, turned her back to him and did what the proud, perhaps foolish Taylor women had perfected as a family art. She turned a blind eye to the humiliation blanketing her and moved on.

To be among such happiness when her heart was so bleak was torturous. The only thing that made it bearable was the thought that in three weeks she'd be following her heart for the first time. Just her. Just Diana.

She wondered what she was going to find when she discovered who she really was.

Coburn's third Scotch had his blood humming through his veins in a heated pull that tempted him to engage with the long-legged thing of beauty who'd once convinced him he needed no other. It was almost irresistible the force that drew him to her, that had always drawn him to her, despite the bitter recrimination he knew she could dish out with that stiff, superior manner of hers. But he resisted. His speech was happening in minutes and he needed all his composure to do it.

He watched Diana circulate through the crowd, her exquisite manners easing every interaction into the perfect sixty seconds of social repartee no matter what the party-goer's background. Diana always knew what to say, even when bent on sticking a dagger into his back.

She was tall for a woman, five foot nine, downplaying her height as usual with a lower heel than most of the females in the room. Her slim boyish figure was the same lithe silhouette, her sensual, exotic features still utterly arresting, but the hair she used to wear well past her shoulders was shorter now, skimming her collarbone. He'd never let her cut it. He'd loved the feel of it sliding against his skin when she'd leaned down to kiss him as she'd taken him inside the tight sheath of her body, always in tune with him at that moment when he filled her completely and wiped any barriers from between them.

As far as makeup sex had gone, and there'd been a lot of it, he and Diana had perfected the art. Hot and filled with a dozen unspoken emotions, it had been a ride he'd become addicted to, until it had destroyed them.

His body reacted to the memory with a tightening his anger could not prevent. Every man at that party in Chelsea the night they'd met had pinpointed his wife as the ultimate conquest. The ice princess who had swept them all with a disdainful look that had said, "Don't bother."

It had been like waving a red flag in front of a bull. He hadn't been able to resist. Diana's quick comebacks and complete lack of awe when it came to him had entranced him. She'd known she was deserving. She'd been *born* deserving. And he'd been up to the challenge. What he wasn't to know at the time was the extent to which her innocence would enslave him with a far greater power than his sexual prowess had claimed her. He hadn't been able to bear the thought of her with another man after he'd taken her, and had put a ring big enough to sink a ship on her finger shortly thereafter to make sure it never happened.

How foolish to think a ring could ever command her complete attention. He hadn't been enough for her. He suspected no man ever would be.

"You ready?" Tony appeared at his side.

He nodded. *A lifetime of happiness.* He was going to wish his friends the best, then shut his mouth. It wasn't that hard.

He waited with Rory and Tony at the front of the room while Annabelle's maid of honor made sure everyone had a glass of Veuve in their hands, courtesy of the Grants. Then he strolled to the center of the room at Tony's nod. The crowd stood gathered around him, a festive cheer in the air at an occasion full of such promise. His eyes picked out Diana in the second row, her gaze carefully averted from his. His blood fizzled in his veins, his prepared speech flying out the window.

"I'm sure you've all heard the joke that love is temporary insanity, cured by marriage." He paused as scattered laughter filled the room. "While I think that is hardly the case with Tony and Annabelle, who are two of the most perfectly matched people I have ever encountered, make no mistake about it," he underscored harshly, "marriage is hard."

The room went so silent you could hear the clinking of swizzle sticks as the bartenders mixed drinks. "Marriage isn't just about finding a person you love," he continued, oblivious to the agitated stare Rory was throwing him, "because I think that *does* happen. I do think falling in love is possible. What's far harder is *staying* in love. Finding someone you can live with. Finding someone whose hopes and dreams, whose ideologies, mirror yours so when the going gets tough, when the inevitable realities of life intrude, that bond has the strength to support you both past the attraction that drew you together."

He paused, the voices in his head warning him to stop, but his heart wouldn't let him. Rory looked panic-stricken now, his gaze imploring him to rein it in. Annabelle was chewing on her lip, staring at him. Tony was frowning with that deliberate calm of his.

Coburn shrugged. "Someone neglected to tell me that you can love a person madly, blindly, but it still isn't going to work if you can't accept each other's flaws and imperfections. That," he added deliberately, looking at Diana, "sometimes love isn't enough."

Diana's dark eyes shone almost black in her chalk-white face. Every party, every social function, every night he'd come home to an empty house flashed through his head in rapid-fire succession to counter the stab of pain that lanced through him.

He removed his gaze from his wife and pinned it on Tony and Annabelle. Tony had an arm around his fiancée's waist now, his expression furious. Coburn dipped his chin.

"All of this to say, sometimes one of those once-in-a-lifetime unions comes along you know will never suffer the fate of others. That you know is the deep and everlasting variety. Tony and Annabelle, I know that you will thrive and prosper together because you are one of those unions. I am so looking forward to watching you grow old together."

The look on Tony's face said their friendship might not last the next ten minutes. He ignored it and lifted his glass. "Here's to Tony and Annabelle, one of the special ones... A lifetime of happiness to you both."

The crowd lifted their glasses in stunned silence. Coburn drank deeply, moved to embrace Tony, who muttered an expletive in his ear, then dropped a kiss on the cheek of a bemused Annabelle, who looked as if she wanted to kill him only slightly less than Tony did. "You might want to address some of those repressed feelings," she suggested drily.

Or not. He stepped back as the couple was surrounded by well-wishers, ignored Rory's scowl and headed for the terrace and some much-needed fresh air. In fact, he thought, perhaps the whole disaster of an evening might lie in breathing the same air as his erstwhile wife.

The crisp, cool late-August night wrapped itself around him like an embrace, a slight breeze teasing the hair at the base of his neck. He yanked his tie looser and undid the top couple of buttons of his shirt. He had been way out of line in there, but some inexplicable force had insisted he tell the truth. And why the *hell* had she chosen tonight to resurface?

High-heeled shoes clicked on the concrete. He didn't have to turn around to know it was Diana. He knew her tread, her gait, how those long legs of hers ate up the distance.

"How *could* you?"

He wheeled to face her. "How could *you*? These are *my* friends."

She came to a halt in front of him. A flush spread across her perfect alabaster skin, staining her cheeks a soft pink. "They're my friends, too. Annabelle asked me to come."

"Then, you should have declined," he said harshly. "You've spent twelve months avoiding me, avoiding anything about us, and you choose *tonight* to resurface?" He shook his head. "Usually your social etiquette is dead-on Diana, but tonight it's been left sorely wanting."

Her eyes darkened into furious black orbs, her fingers clutching her evening bag tight. "I would say *your* social etiquette is what's lacking tonight, Coburn. First your insulting throwaway comment everyone heard, then your telling speech about how much you hated being married to me."

"What?" he drawled mockingly. "You didn't like the joke? I thought it particularly apt given our present situation, because it certainly was insanity what we shared. Or perhaps you didn't like me suggesting you have flaws? Letting the world in on your dirty little secret?"

"No," she said slowly, the flush in her cheeks descending to stain her chest with a matching rosy hue. "Your poor taste in the speech I can take, although I'm sure Tony and Annabelle won't be thanking you later. It was your inappropriate comment to Rory I thought excessively juvenile."

"You mean the one about being over a smart mouth and a great body?" His mouth twisted. "Really, Di, that could have been about anyone. Although," he conceded, raking his gaze over her lithe body and small, high breasts, "it certainly does ring true in your case."

His bald-faced lie had her clenching her free hand at her side. "You're still a bastard, Coburn Grant. That hasn't changed, either."

"Sorry, no." He watched as his perusal elicited the agitated response it always did in her, turning the rosy hue in her skin a dark red and sending the pulse at the base of her neck fluttering. "You could have avoided it by showing up at our meeting tomorrow and not among my closest circle of friends."

She exhaled on a long sigh. "You won't have to worry about me being around much longer. You can have New York all to yourself."

His gaze sharpened on her face. "What does that mean?"

"I'm leaving in three and a half weeks to join Doctors Without Borders in Africa."

"*Africa?* What about the job you are so in love with you couldn't find time for me?"

"I left." Her chin rose, gaze tangling with his. "I decided our divorce was the perfect opportunity to wipe the slate clean."

He studied the mutinous set of her full mouth. "*You* left your job?"

"Yes."

He was unprepared for the searing pain that sliced through him. *Now* when they were about to end their marriage with two signatures on a piece of paper she'd done the one thing that might have saved them. "Why?" he bit out, his hand clenching tight around his champagne glass. "Don't tell me…you needed to *find* yourself."

Her chin lifted another notch. "Something like that."

He was at a true loss as to where to go with that information. All he'd ever wanted was for them to have time to devote to each other. For her to act like his true partner. But she'd never allowed it. She had refused to pull back on her grueling schedule, which had once seen her home only two days in a month as a resident, claiming it would impact her career.

"Forgive me," he said finally, "if the whole idea of this confounds me at this particular moment."

Her long lashes fanned over her pale cheeks. "It's time one of us grew up, Coburn. And since that clearly isn't going to be you with your floozy-a-week love life, I guess it has to be me."

He absorbed the insult like a boxer taking a misguided, poorly aimed punch. "You never could get past them could you, Di? What was history never was for you."

She opened her eyes, an amber glint firing amid a mahogany canvas. "Hard when it was thrown in my face every second minute. Why do you think I stopped attending parties with you? Who could stomach knowing that half the women in the room had had my husband?"

"You mentioned that before," he countered, enjoying the fact he was getting to her. "A complete exaggeration I'll tell you once again. You made me a mythological figure in your head, Di. None of it bore anything close to reality."

"It's hard to separate the fool's gold from the real thing," she scoffed. "I suppose you will have to tone it down now that you are lording it as CEO. Are you sure your ego can handle all the power?"

"It's in fine shape," he murmured on a low warning as he bent his head to her. "And thank you for the sincere congratulations on my promotion."

She moistened her lips as he impaled her with his gaze. His satisfaction at how he still got to her knew no bounds. "Perhaps we should continue this discussion somewhere else? Rather than hijacking the happy occasion any more than we already have?"

"I—I don't think that's a good idea." Her gaze dropped to the skin exposed by his unbuttoned shirt. "I should go anyway. I have a ton of things to do before I leave."

He closed his hand around her slim wrist. "I disagree," he countered in a silky-soft tone. "This is a discussion we should have had twelve months ago. Why not have it now before you run off to prove to your father you have a mind of your own?"

"And you." The words tumbled out of her mouth before she censored herself.

He watched dismay cloud them. "Yes, Di," he bit out. *"Exactly that."*

Ebony eyes bound to blue. Emotion, something he couldn't remember seeing in her for the last interminably painful year they'd spent together, flared in the eyes staring back at him. It made something elemental fire inside him. This was his chance to scratch beneath the surface of his wife. And although that was the last thing he should be doing the night before they ended their relationship with a resoundingly civilized divorce settlement, it was a temptation his white-hot curiosity couldn't resist.

"We're leaving," he muttered, wrapping his fingers firmer around her wrist and pulling her toward the French doors.

She tugged on his arm. "You're making a scene."

"Not as much as we've made already." He directed her toward their hosts and the happy couple to say their goodbyes. Eyes followed them as they went, sending regret lancing through him. Tonight had once again proved his wife brought out the worst in him. It was time to put an end to it once and for all—an end that had nothing to do with paperwork.

CHAPTER TWO

DIANA TOOK THE glass of water her husband handed to her, closing her shaky fingers tight around the tumbler so he wouldn't see how nervous she was. The tension that had been screaming through her ever since she'd entered Coburn's beautifully decorated bachelor pad just a couple of blocks from the party was threatening to annihilate her composure.

She walked out onto the glazed concrete terrace while Coburn found a bottle of wine. The large open space with its comfortable lounge furniture scattered throughout was easily as big as the square footage of his trendy penthouse apartment on the top floor of the Chelsea low-rise—casual elegance that reflected her husband's free-spirited need to be outdoors as much as possible.

Moving to the edge of the terrace that overlooked the tree-lined street, elegant with its neat little brick buildings and wrought iron fences, she rested her forearms on the railing. The hip neighborhood fit her husband's persona to a T—notable, relaxed while still possessing enough individuality that he wouldn't feel stifled as he had in their impossibly expensive, old-money East Side co-op.

A party was in full swing on the rooftop terrace of the building opposite, the loud dance music carrying on the air to where she stood. She set the glass down on the ledge before the water sloshed over the side. Why had she let her husband railroad her into coming here? Hadn't they said all they needed to say in that final blowout that had put any of the ones before it to shame? Hadn't she walked out on him because that night it had become crystal clear they weren't going to make it together? That what they'd had had died and all they were doing was torturing each other?

She closed her eyes. She could still feel the force of her husband's anger blanketing her even now. He had walked in from a party just as she had returned home from a shift at the hospital, the blood staining her wrists she'd missed in her final scrub a testament to her exhaustion. Coburn had been out for a fight from the minute he'd tossed his jacket on a chair and she'd known it, known she should just retreat into the shower and let him cool off. But his furious tirade had been off and running by then. People were starting to talk about her continued absence at social functions, he'd told her. Rumors were circulating about the state of their marriage. Questioning whether they would last… *I've had enough of it, Di. Enough of this half-life with you.*

She'd somehow found the energy to fight back because none of what he was saying was fair. Just because her husband enjoyed giving his older brother fits by taking off for a last-minute bicycle race in the French Riviera didn't mean she had the same lack of loyalty to *her* job. People's lives depended on her. She didn't get to choose when and how long she was on duty. But Coburn in his stubborn arrogance had stated there were other doctors in the city of Manhattan, and *he* needed her by his side. Which had devolved into him suggesting she was using her work to avoid him and their issues. Which might have had some truth to it. But she had been too mad, too hurt to rein in her arsenal of similar complaints about his irresponsible behavior. Where had he been the night of the Taylor holiday party when she'd needed him by *her* side? Partying in Cannes with friends…

They'd traded barbs until she literally couldn't stand on two feet anymore, then she'd showered and spent the night in the spare bedroom. The next day she'd moved into her parents' guest room until she could find an apartment of her own. Coburn had been too angry to come after her. Maybe all there was to be said had been said.

Her father had gleefully offered an "I told you so" and beat Coburn's shortcomings into her head until she was sufficiently brainwashed she knew she would never go back. But in the spirit of her newfound brutally honest outlook on life, as painful as it might be, she knew her father couldn't be blamed for her and Coburn's split. They had needed no assistance wrecking the good that they'd had.

The fact that Coburn had been with other women months after they'd parted had been the final nail in the coffin. The part of her that had held out hope they might work things out had died then.

The only mystery was why neither of them had filed the divorce papers sooner. It had been she, after signing her contract to work abroad, who had started the proceedings.

A chorus of excited giggles floated across the air to her as a group of girls horsed around with two attractive males. *You aren't fun anymore.* Coburn's words echoed through her head from that last night. *What happened to you?*

She thought about it. Had she ever been fun? Being a resident was not meant to be a joyride. It had been the most grueling five years of her life, meant to separate the weak from the strong. Why couldn't her husband have accepted the early years were going to be like that? That it *would* change.

He joined her on the terrace then, as if she'd conjured him up to ask just that question. But of course she hadn't. Not now when they were about to make their relationship history.

She eyed the bottle of champagne in his hands. "What are we celebrating?"

His sensuous mouth curved in a humorless smile. "How about our incredibly civilized divorce?"

Her mouth twisted. "Because the lawyers hashed out every clause for us."

"Your decision." His electric blue eyes lanced through her. "I was willing to sit down and act like two reasonable human beings for an hour. *You* for some reason were not. I'm very curious as to why that might be."

She hadn't let herself wonder that. Perhaps because she didn't want to know the answer.

She watched the play of muscles in his forearms as he worked the cork out of the bottle. Exposed by his rolled-up sleeves, they were one of her favorite parts of him. Lean and muscular, he was all sinewy power without an excess centimeter of flesh on him. Potently strong enough to brace himself with as he flipped her from one sexual position to the next…

The cork flew into the air with a decisive pop. It jerked her back to reality. She couldn't be thinking things like that. Thoughts like that had always gotten her into trouble when it came to Coburn. Because they inevitably led to sex and their erotic, spectacular love life that had become a crutch for their utterly dismal relationship skills.

Coburn filled two glasses and handed one to her, his gaze resting on her heated cheeks. "Disconcerting, isn't it, probing at the real reasons why we do the things we do? Maybe you were scared that one hour in a boardroom would end up the way it always does with us… You would call me a selfish son of a bitch and I would make you eat your words, one orgasm at a time."

The heat in her cheeks darkened into a full-out fire. "Perhaps my choice was the wiser one, then?"

"Or the coward's way out."

Her chin lifted. "There's nothing wrong with a bit of self-realization. In not repeating the same mistakes we've made in the past..."

"If you call that part of our relationship a mistake, yes." The glitter in his gaze made her shift her weight to the other foot. *Damn* but this had been a colossal mistake.

He lifted his glass, his gaze holding hers. "To self-realization, then. *And* the dissolution of our hasty, ill-thought-out vows."

A throb dug itself deep into her flesh, somewhere in the region of her heart. To hear him sum up their union like that without acknowledging the intense highs only they had offered each other didn't seem right. "To greater self-realization," she echoed, lifting the glass to her lips.

"What?" he murmured after he'd taken a sip. "You don't agree we were a hasty, ill-thought-out union?"

She turned her head to look at the revelers. "I think we were much more than that."

A silence fell between them. She felt his eyes on her, coolly assessing. When she thought he might say something, she cut him off at the pass. "I'm happy for Harrison. He'll make a fine president if he wins."

"The country couldn't do any better."

"And Frankie. She's very beautiful." A cynical note entered her voice as she referenced her husband's PA, who was married to his older brother. "How did you let that one get away? She is so your type, Coburn. Young and impressionable."

"And about to give up her career for her and Harrison's new addition to the family." His mouth curled with a sardonic twist. "What a lucky man he is... He married a woman who doesn't need to prove herself to the world."

The dagger cut through her as cleanly as her own surgeon's scalpel. "You never seemed to want babies, Coburn. If that was high on your list, you should have mentioned it when you were cataloging my potential as your wife. You knew with my residency it would be years."

A frown furrowed his brow. "There was no *cataloging*. We married before we had any idea who the other one was."

Her stomach knotted. "And you found me sorely lacking in any capacity other than the bedroom."

His gaze narrowed. "You liked to think that was the reason. Because then you didn't have to work at it at all. You could just run off like the spoiled little rich girl you were and cry to Daddy. There were no repercussions."

No repercussions? She'd spent the past year trying to bury herself in her work because it was too painful to go home to an apartment that didn't have Coburn in it. He really had no clue.

"You think I'm the only one who's unknowable?" she offered quietly. "I could do an entire emotional autopsy on you, Coburn, and I would still never get to the bottom of you. You play like you're so open and there, but none of it is the real you."

His eyes glittered. "You have to give some to get some, Di."

Right. Here they were at the same old discussion. A waste of time.

"Why didn't you file for divorce? You were certainly anxious to move on and avail yourself of other female company."

He lifted a shoulder. "I don't plan to marry again so there was so rush. And as for my sexual partners? My prerogative when you ended our marriage. You know I have a high level of *need*."

A need that had apparently overwhelmed him within months of their marriage ending…

She lifted her gaze and watched the midnight blue sky streaked with a swath of purple swallow up a lone star.

Her insides hurt, like the delicate, shaky aftermath of a horrible flu.

"How long will you be gone?"

Coburn was watching her with that all-seeing gaze of his. "Three months, maybe more. The need for surgeons is critical."

"What happened to your dream of working with Moritz?"

"I couldn't handle the politics." Swiss surgeon Frank Moritz was one of the most revered pediatric surgeons in the world, a specialty she wanted to make her own, but as Diana had found out, he was also one of the biggest egos in the profession. She had impressed him enough to put herself in line for the fellowship he was offering, but she hadn't been able to force herself to do the schmoozing being Moritz's choice entailed. It went against every belief she had that talent should prevail.

He lifted a brow. "You knew that was going to be part of it."

"I didn't know it was going to color *every aspect* of it. The man is a megalomaniac."

"So you're just giving up your career?"

"No. I'm going to Africa to practice."

He waved his glass at her. "You know what I mean. You will be out of the loop. You'll have to start all over again."

"So be it." A wry smile curved her lips. "It's done, Coburn. I've sold my apartment and my car. I need to find my way."

He studied her as if she was a creature from a different species he'd come into contact with. And maybe she was. She wasn't the same Diana who'd walked away from him, that was for sure. She'd done far too much soul-searching to be that.

"Don't you think it's a bit drastic to put yourself in the middle of a war-torn country to find yourself? If it's me you're trying to avoid, then move to another state. Move to another country, for God's sake. Not a *war zone*."

She straightened her shoulders, her lips flattening into a stubborn line. "This isn't about you, Coburn. Things aren't always about you, although you like to think they are. This is about *me* and my need to help other people with the skills I have."

His gaze narrowed on her. "You forget you admitted to me earlier part of this is you thumbing your nose at me."

Damn her loose mouth. She sunk her teeth into her lower lip. "That was a knee-jerk reaction to an old wound. Nothing you say or do affects me anymore."

"Then, why do you avoid me? You've been systematically ensuring our paths don't cross for the past year." He lifted a brow. "How do I know this? Because every time I'm unable to make something, I hear afterward you were miraculously able to attend. That's a lot of trouble to go to to avoid someone whose presence doesn't *affect* you."

She swallowed hard, studying the play of light over his achingly familiar face. She had been avoiding him, of course, but it wasn't something she was ever going to admit.

"So I ask again," he demanded roughly, "why show up tonight? What purpose did this serve?"

Standing this close to him, inhaling his spicy aftershave mixed with a fresh citrus lime that had always made her weak in the knees, she suffered the horrifying realization that maybe it was closure she had wanted. One more chance to see him before she signed those papers. One more chance to put this demon to rest before she put her life behind her for a future that was a complete unknown. To convince herself she was doing the right thing by walking away from him. Instead, all she could think about was his horrible, hurtful comment to Rory.

I'm not twenty-five anymore. An amazing body and a smart mouth don't do it for me any longer.

Was that all she'd ever been to him?

She tilted her head back and looked up at him. "You didn't mean what you said to Rory."

His mouth compressed into a straight line. "Oh, but I did, Diana. I may still *want* you because you have an undeniably sweet body I could spend my life sinking myself into. But as for any emotion beyond that? History, sweetheart. You made sure of that."

The hollow feeling that consumed her then was frightening in its intensity. She could not sign those papers tomorrow, could not step on that plane knowing that was what he thought of her. That she wasn't any different from all of his other women. That what they had had meant nothing.

She moved closer until the tips of her breasts brushed against the fine material of his shirt and her hips were cradled in the wide breadth of his. His heat moved through her, reminding her just how good it felt to be held against him.

"What were those women to you?" she asked, tracing a finger over the groove at the side of his mouth that seemed to have grown deeper. "A salve for your embittered soul? A way to prove I meant so little to you?"

He captured her hand in his. "I just told you, Di, I'm over you. Don't give yourself so much credit."

But she could feel his arousal stirring to life against her. Feel the rigidness of his powerful body with every contact point it shared with hers. Sex had never just been about the physical between them—it had transcended that, branded them with a truth they couldn't deny. And she wanted it. *Now.* Then she could walk away.

She ran her free hand up the hard muscles of his thigh

until she found the essence of his virility. His rough intake of breath sent a surge of satisfaction through her.

"What the hell are you doing?"

She lifted her gaze to his. "Maybe I came tonight for this. Maybe we should finish it like we started..."

Hot color stained his cheeks, the cords of his muscular neck standing out in stark definition. "I think that's a bad idea."

Her fingers traced the hard ridge of him along the zipper of his pants. His response was instantaneous, his flesh swelling beneath her touch. It set her blood on fire to prove she could still affect him like this.

He arched his hips to press himself into her hand. "This is just sex."

She closed her fingers more firmly around him. "Whatever you say."

"Diana." His fingers captured her jaw, tilting her face up to his. "This means *nothing*. Know that if I take you now."

But she saw the emotion raging in his eyes. Knew it from their navy blue color so dark now his pupils blended with their inky depths. He was lying.

She reached for his belt buckle. His big body tensed beneath her fingers and for a long excruciating moment, she thought he would reject her. Then he dropped his hands, his gaze sinking into hers.

"You want one more night, Di? I can do that."

A wave of adrenaline rolled through her, so strong, so powerful she was incapable of resisting it. It was so wrong but so right to be with him like this, but the right was, oh, so much stronger. Her hands worked his belt out of the buckle and yanked it free. His zipper accommodated her downward movement with a sharp hiss that made her stomach clench. Then there was only his hard, hot flesh to rediscover. He was silk over iron power, thick and unforgiving, and he knew exactly how to use it.

His groan split the night air. "There is a party going on thirty feet away."

She squeezed her fingers around his burgeoning flesh. "I thought you liked to walk on the wild side…"

"Not with people I pass on the street every day."

But his protest was halfhearted. His back was to the railing, shielding him from the revelers. His body was tense, expectant beneath her fingers, his flesh responding to her touch, pulsing, growing under her caress until he lay erect against his abdomen.

If he didn't touch her soon, she was going to scream.

A hand clamped over hers. His face when she looked up at him was full of such heated intent it stopped her heart in her chest. "You know I'm not a taker like that."

She did. She knew what a thorough, giving, wildly erotic lover he was, and maybe that had been half the problem tonight. She wanted that—soul destroying or otherwise.

She dropped her hands to her sides as he peeled the straps of her dress from her shoulders and cupped her naked flesh. It felt so good to have his hands on her after so long, she let out a low moan and arched into him. He bent and closed his mouth over a taut peak and sucked hard, his sudden assault on her body thrilling. His lips and teeth were insistent, unrelenting, demanding a response from the very core of her. "You like that," he muttered against her flesh. "You always liked that."

She moaned something like a response. He worked the nipple between his fingers as he transferred his attention to the other, sucking and pulling at her until the ache in her abdomen was so acute she thought he might bring her to orgasm with this alone. Her hips moved restlessly against him, demanding more. He moved his palm to her buttock, cupped her and held her in place against his arousal. For a long moment, she was suspended in a starry corridor that promised heaven. Then he gave it to her, the rhythmic pull of his mouth on her nipple sending a sweet surge of pleasure through her limbs that pulled a cry from her lips.

This, this was why it had only ever been Coburn.

Coburn watched his wife come down from her orgasm, her delicate face flushed with pleasure. The fact that he could make her come with just his mouth and the right amount of friction satisfied him on a level he couldn't even begin to understand. This was when his wife was *his*. When they were perfect together.

He ran his hands up the inside of her filmy party dress and found her thong. The thin side ripped easily, pulling away from her skin like the unwanted impediment it was. Diana's eyes rounded.

"That's right, wife," he growled. "You have me in a particular kind of mood."

She didn't resist as he turned her around so her back was against the railing, her body shielding him from the partygoers. His mouth settled against the shell of her ear. "Spread your legs."

She resisted for a moment at the authoritative tone behind the command. Then her muscles relaxed beneath his hands as he moved her thighs apart and found what he was looking for. Hot responsive silk that had the ability to make him forget every rational thought he'd ever had.

She went rigid beneath his touch but not to stop him. She threw her head back, exposing her irresistible long, slim neck, and reveled in it. He buried his lips in her floral scent and moved his fingers against her in a slow, languid caress.

"Oh, God."

His wife had always been responsive, but this time he

savored every sigh, every moan, every delicate whimper as he brushed his thumb against the nub at the center of her. Worked it slowly, deliberately until she was moving against his hand, his name a whispered plea that did something to his battered soul.

"You have always been mine. *Always.*"

She didn't respond. She didn't have to. He knew the truth, knew the power they held over each other. It pushed him forward, goaded him on as he slid a finger inside her in a caress he knew she loved. Her eyes closed; her hips worked against his hand. Her breathing was fractured, hitched in the night air, her body trembling beneath his hands as she stood poised to shatter into another release. But he wasn't going to give it to her that way.

He withdrew his fingers from her. Her eyes flew open. "There will be no audience," he said roughly.

He slid his arms under her knees, picked her up and strode through the apartment to his bedroom. It was a big mistake to take her there, he knew. If he did, he would never get her out of his head. It was *his* bed, *his* space he'd created when she'd left him hollow and broken. To let her violate it again was surely unwise, but he wasn't thinking with his head—he was thinking with another body part entirely.

The play of the moonlight through the skylight was all he needed to absorb his wife's jaw-dropping beauty as he deposited her on the bed. She was everything he'd ever wanted, everything he could no longer let himself want. Not after this.

He stripped off his pants, shirt and tie and slid on a condom. Diana was staring at him as if he was a beast on the prowl, and he liked that. Liked when she was at his mercy. He straddled her, pinning her to the bed with his heavier weight. She looked brazen with her dress half-off and her eyes full of desire. He ran a hand from her throat to the heat between her legs, pushing her dress up to her waist. Her lips parted in an unspoken message. The urge to kiss her, to take possession of her sultry full mouth, was so strong it nearly consumed him. He swallowed it back, clamped his jaw down hard on the need. If he did that, this bedroom would never be his own.

"Coburn?" Diana lifted her hand to curve around his nape. Her dark eyes were confused, questioning. He closed his against the emotion he saw there because now it was too much for him. Now it threatened to singe him beyond repair. He allowed her fingers to bring his head down toward her parted lips, but at the last minute he turned his head and buried his mouth in her throat. She went rigid beneath him. He captured her nipple in his mouth to distract her, his hand moving down her stomach to ready her silken flesh for him. The stiffness left her on a low, reluctant moan.

That was when he took her with a powerful, driving thrust. She accommodated him easily. She had been built to take him. He had to close his eyes to hang on to the moment, to focus on the pleasure drawing the act out would bring both of them, or he would have been lost, she felt that exquisitely good. Like returning to heaven.

That last thought in particular drove him forward, a mixture of anger and need behind his powerful thrusts. He slid his palms under her hips to take it deeper, until she squeezed her eyes shut and he knew it was so good for her it was almost too much. He slowed it down then, gentled his movements despite the emotion raging in his blood. When she relaxed beneath him, he angled her hips with his palms and stroked to that place inside her that gave her the deepest, most satisfying release. Her body clenched around him, reaching for it.

"Please."

"Look at me."

She opened her eyes. They were glazed, drunk with the promise of ecstasy. He gripped her hips more firmly with his hands and moved inside her with deliberate, pleasure-inducing strokes designed to give her release. When she came, he saw the whole thing happen in her ebony eyes.

He waited until her breathing slowed, her eyes cleared and she was fully with him before he sought his release. He wanted her to remember every minute, every second of this when she was with someone else, when some other man claimed her beautiful body and he was relegated to a footnote in her life.

He wanted it to be so good he'd ruin her for anyone else. Wanted her to know the agony of wanting something you couldn't have.

Her eyes fluttered open to stare into his. He wrapped one of her long, elegant legs around his waist and took her with deliberate, deep insistent strokes that dismantled any last bit of composure he saw on her beautiful face. When it became too good, too exquisite to take, he arched his back and let the release consume him. His brain faded to black. Nothing but the pleasure raging through him could touch him.

He lay there, supporting part of his weight on his palms until he recovered himself. Diana's satiny limbs were wrapped around him, her scent filling his nostrils. Long moments later, when his breath had come back, he registered her stillness beneath him. Levering himself off her, he studied her stricken face. She had expected this to change everything as it always had. She had expected to crack his shell.

He rolled off her and swung his legs over the side of the bed. Fury sizzled through his blood as he stood up and stared down at her. "Was that a good enough performance for the memory book? Or should we do it again?"

Her face lost all its color. She sat up and pulled her

dress down to cover her. "No," she said slowly, "that was perfect."

"Good." He waved a hand at the shower. "I'm going to clean up. Feel free to join me."

But she didn't. He knew she wouldn't. When he emerged from the shower ten minutes later, she was gone, just as she'd been gone the last time. He took one look at the bed, threw on some clothes and walked out into the dark, quiet night. If he'd thought it would feel good, this victory over her, it didn't. It felt as if he'd just impaled himself on his own sword.

Diana wasn't sure how she got to Beth's house. Didn't even know she was crying until she'd pulled her keys out on her friend's doorstep and was fumbling while trying to get them into the lock, her gaze too blurred to see. Her palm pressed against the door as she jammed the key in harder. The door opened from the inside, sending her tumbling across the jamb.

"Sweetheart." Beth caught her forearms and steadied her. "What's wrong?"

The tears turned into a torrent, sliding down her cheeks unchecked. "I am s-so s-stupid."

Beth pulled the door shut, retrieved her keys and guided her into the cozy little living room. "You saw him, I take it?"

She choked back a sob at that vast understatement of what had just happened. She had just had steamy, intensely uninhibited sex with her soon-to-be ex, who'd tossed her aside afterward as if she meant nothing to him.

Beth's lips tightened. "I'm getting us some tea, then we talk."

Diana kicked off her shoes, curled up on the sofa and grabbed the box of tissues sitting on the coffee table. Images from the night flew at her like jagged pieces of a puzzle that didn't make any sense in her head. She hadn't consciously gone to that party tonight to have that showdown with Coburn, but it was clear now that unconsciously she had. Her heart hadn't mended since that night she'd walked out on him. She still wasn't over him, and worse, she'd been holding out some hope he might still love her.

A sitcom Beth had been watching blared from the TV. She sat watching it with unseeing eyes. Had she been hoping Coburn would confess he felt the same way? That that was the real reason he hadn't initiated a divorce?

She swallowed hard. What a stupid, blind woman she was. She had set herself up for that tonight. Set herself up for Coburn's masterful demonstration of just how little he cared. Because after what he'd just done to her? Those flashes of emotion she'd thought she'd seen in his eyes must had been figments of her imagination. Evidence she'd used to justify the need to be in his arms again. Because being without him had been as if a part of her was missing and she couldn't seem to get it back.

Was that a good enough performance for the memory book? Or should we do it again?

His brutal words ripped at her insides. Bile rose in her throat. She might have been sick if she'd had anything more than a couple of hors d'oeuvres in her stomach. She swallowed the nausea down, pushing it away. How had she let herself do that after a whole year of telling herself she couldn't be anywhere near him? Where had the measured rationality she was known for in her work been when she needed it most?

Beth came back, handing her a steaming mug of her favorite peppermint tea. Her best friend since med school sat down on the other end of the sofa with her own mug of tea. "Tell me what happened."

Diana pushed her disheveled hair out of her face and gave her nose one last swipe. "I saw him and I was so ready to be cool and composed, and then I just— I mean—" She let out a long sigh. "I'm still in love with him."

Her friend grimaced. "And there's a newsflash."

She pressed her hands to her temples. "He gave this toast to Annabelle and Tony that ended up being all about us and, God, it was awful. Everyone was staring at us."

Beth's eyes rounded. "He did *not*."

She nodded. "Then he insisted on going back to his apartment and talking."

"What is there to talk about? You two are getting divorced tomorrow."

"He was angry. He accused me of running away from our problems. He said I was a spoiled little rich girl who'd run back to Daddy when the going got tough." She threw her friend a despairing look. "But honestly, how many more times could we argue about the same things? It was getting toxic."

"You tried, Di." Beth's gaze softened. "I watched you try, I watched you suffer, but you are just two very different people with very different ideas of what you want out of life."

And *that* was the crux of it. It was why she'd left. Her husband's brutal summation of their marriage echoed in her ears, the matter-of-fact, cynical tone he'd uttered it in making her cringe all over again. "In his speech," she said huskily, "he said that someone forgot to tell him that sometimes love isn't enough. That you can love someone madly, blindly, but it still isn't going to work if you can't accept each other's flaws and imperfections."

Beth leaned forward and clasped her hands. "He's right. Sometimes love isn't enough. Sometimes the passionate, intense affairs like you and he have had are the hardest to sustain. They just don't lend themselves to ordinary life."

A fresh wave of tears pooled at the back of her eyes. A part of her didn't want to accept that that could be possible with her and Coburn. But the rational, self-preservative side of her said she must.

Beth squeezed her hands tighter. "I was in the room the night you and Coburn met. I remember what it was like watching you two… It was *electric*. But that kind of passion? It can blind you to reality."

A reality she had to accept now. Coburn didn't love her anymore and she had to move on. If it had been closure she'd been looking for as she walked away from everything she knew, tonight he'd given it to her. As brutal as it had been, Coburn had actually done her a favor.

"You're right," she said, grabbing another tissue and blowing her nose. Pushing her shoulders back, she gave her best friend a decisive look. "This was the eye-opener I needed to walk into that meeting tomorrow and do what I need to do."

Maybe when she was thousands of miles away from Coburn she might somehow be able to banish the shame she'd felt tonight when he'd looked at her as if he'd just finished servicing another of his bimbos. Because if she didn't, she might hate him forever.

CHAPTER THREE

"WELL, THAT WAS REFRESHING."

Coburn ignored the sarcasm in his older brother's voice and kept walking toward the elevators. The board meeting had run long and he was late for his meeting with Diana and the lawyers.

"Don't get me wrong," Harrison continued, keeping step with him, "I love how progressive you're being. God knows we need a more flexible vacation policy, but how do you think it's going to work when all our employees decide to take the same day off? We have critical processes on the supply-chain side."

"That won't happen." Coburn threw him an annoyed glance. "Employment experts have done studies on it, and it's clear in most workforces self-ownership of deadlines will regulate all that."

"And self-regulation will be top of mind when the Christmas holidays hit?" Harrison frowned. "You saw the board in there. You're pushing hard and fast to make changes here, Coburn. You have a different vision, a different style of leadership. But you need to let them catch up with you."

"They will." He jabbed the call button for the elevator. "And they'll be thanking me when our employee satisfaction and productivity numbers are up."

"If they don't revolt first."

He gave his brother a quelling look. "I thought you were going to let me run this company my way."

"That was before you started spouting nonsense about no formal vacation policy and the need for badge levels to incent employees. This isn't a video game we're playing. It's a Fortune 500 company our family has spent a hundred years building."

"I get that." He stepped on the empty arriving elevator and Harrison followed. He got the pressure that was on him. He got that he was following his godlike brother in the analysts' eyes. He got all of it until he was sick to death of it.

Harrison shook his head at him. "You make me nervous."

"Don't be." He pushed the button for the executive floor. "Focus on your campaign. Shake people's hands, pretend their babies are cute. I've got this."

The elevator swished upward, revealing a panoramic view of New York. A long silence followed. "Are you sure," Harrison ventured carefully when he eventually broke it, "your emotions aren't a little...*off* with this divorce on your plate?"

Coburn glanced at his watch. "Happening in minutes. In fact, I'm fifteen of them late."

"That doesn't answer my question." His brother exhaled on a long sigh. "She'd kill me if she knew I was saying this, but Frankie says you haven't been yourself lately."

"I have a lot on my mind."

Harrison fixed him with that trademark deadly stare of his. "Do you still care for her?"

And wasn't that the question of the day? He'd told himself he didn't, had convinced himself he was long over his marital fling. But last night had proved him an exemplarity liar. To hijack his toast to Tony and Annabelle with that speech that had come out of nowhere? To sleep with the woman he was intent on wiping from his memory to bring some closure to that part of his life? *Insanity.*

"I am over her," he told his brother, hoping that saying it out loud would make it so. "Making this divorce official is exactly what I need to move on."

His brother's gaze raked his face. "Good. I hope it gives you some perspective."

"To what?" He and his brother were gradually restoring the close relationship that had defined their younger years after a decade of being at odds with each other following their father's death. But lately Harrison's preachiness was rankling him. "Do you think I should settle down like you and have the beautiful little nuclear family? You know how much that appeals to me."

"Actually," his brother drawled, "I was thinking more along the lines of what will make *you* happy. I don't think you have been for a long time, Coburn, and I'm not just talking professionally. Climbing an avalanche-prone mountain is not thrill-seeking—it's self-destructive."

Yes, but on those truly brutal parts of the climb when his limbs felt as if they were going to fall off and he was so cold he thought he might expire, his head had felt devoid of anything, numb to the pure satisfaction of what he'd accomplished. It was addictive.

He lifted a shoulder. "My mountain-climbing days are over if the board has anything to say about it, so your worries are null and void there."

His wife's walk on the dangerous side? Not so much. He'd be lying if he said he hadn't come home and done an internet search on the African country she was going to be working in after his hour-and-a-half-long walk through the streets of Chelsea last night. What he'd found he hadn't liked. Diana was putting herself well within the reach of the rebels who were causing havoc for the government.

Who were known to use kidnapping as a bargaining tactic. He hadn't slept a wink.

Harrison turned to face him as they stepped off the elevator. "Use this time to figure out what you want out of your life. We only do this once. You have a fresh start to work with."

He lifted his chin and met his brother's stare. "Since when did you get so philosophic?"

"Since my wife got hold of me," Harrison admitted with a rueful smile. "I like it, actually..."

Coburn watched him walk away. Now that the aliens had taken his older brother and replaced him with *that* man, he thought maybe he'd consider his point as he strode toward Frankie, who gave the conference room Diana and the lawyers occupied a pointed nod. It was true. A fresh start was exactly what he wanted out of this divorce, and it was exactly what he was going to get. *Now.*

"So sorry," he murmured, striding into the glass-and-chrome conference room with its magnificent views of New York. He kept his gaze firmly away from his soon-to-be ex-wife and on the stiff, expensively suited lawyers who were five hundred an hour apiece.

Chance Hamilton, his lawyer, made an awkward joke about this divorce not going anywhere. Jerry Simmons, Diana's very proper, blue-blooded Harvard grad, stood and shook his hand. His wife remained seated, her eyes fixed on the windows. His guts twisted. She wouldn't even look at him.

"So," Jerry began as Coburn sat down beside Chance, across from Diana, "shall we do a final review of the terms, starting with property?" Diana, who looked like something out of Madame Tussauds wax museum, moved her lips in what he assumed was agreement.

"Fine." He added his assent as he continued to study his wife, despite his better instincts. Only Diana could look her most beautiful in a simple white shirt, slim dark jeans and a floral scarf. Her dramatic dark features and hair made adornment unnecessary, something he'd always found vastly appealing versus the made-up showpieces he came across at most of the social functions he attended.

Her beautiful hair was caught up in a knot today as opposed to last night's wavy curls, her makeup minimal, designed to cover the shadows beneath her eyes, but it hadn't quite worked. Hands that lay in her lap, constantly clenching and unclenching, were the only sign that she felt anything at all.

Last night she had felt a whole hell of a lot. The half-moons dug into his biceps he'd noticed when he'd put on his shirt this morning bore testament to that. The sensation of her body tightening around his as he'd driven her to the brink was burned into his brain, taunting him, reminding him of just how good it was between them.

"The Key West house," Jerry prompted.

Coburn gave him a distracted look. "Sorry?"

"The Key West house. Diana keeps it."

He nodded.

"The East Side apartment closes this week. Half of those proceeds will go to each of you when that happens."

He nodded. He'd hated that apartment from the first day they'd moved in. It had been a stuffy, cliquey building with a tiny terrace that had made him feel like a caged animal. He'd been thrilled to get out of it.

Jerry wrapped up the remainder of their properties and moved on to the incidentals.

"The season tickets to the ballet and the opera will go to Diana, while the basketball tickets go to you, Coburn."

"Fine." Did she really think he wanted to attend a brutally boring opera now that they were through? The only reason he'd ever agreed to go was because watching the joy it put in his wife's eyes when she finally took a night off had been worth it and ten times more.

He nodded. Waved for him to continue.

Jerry started listing off such minor, inconsequential stuff his mind faded to black. What the hell did he care if he had the country club membership? He'd never have time to golf. He also had no interest in the artwork Diana had walked off with.

"I only want the painting of the Pyrenees," he broke in. "She can have the rest."

He'd cycled a race there. It had sentimental value to him.

Jerry nodded and resumed the exhaustive list. Coburn couldn't believe he and Diana had accumulated so much *stuff* in two years. The free spirit in him thought it utterly ridiculous. He waved a hand at Jerry. "She can have it all. Whatever's on the list, let her take it."

He needed to get out of this room *now*.

Jerry looked thrown. "Okay—just give me a moment. I'll move on with the life insurance policies and retirement savings." He started flipping pages. Coburn blew out a breath, stood up and walked to the windows. This whole thing was ridiculous, *insane*. He and Diana both had enough money individually to never have to worry about their financials. He was seriously thinking of making his will out to a nature organization for when he eventually left this world.

He turned and leaned back against the windowsill, his gaze moving to his wife. She was still sitting there frozen, as if she was on another planet. He had the vicious urge to do something to shake her out of it.

"We'll start with the life insurance policies. You—"

"Enough." He waved a hand at Jerry. The lawyer set the paper down with a slow movement, both of the legal experts absorbing his aggressive tone and stance. He pinned his gaze on his wife's face. "Diana, are you all right?"

She lifted her chin, her dark eyes flaring with emotion for the first time. "Perfect."

Exactly what she'd said to him last night after he'd taken her apart with his despicable behavior.

Jerry eyed him. "Should we continue?"

"No." He kept his gaze trained on Diana. "The agreement is fine, all of it. I, however, am not ready to sign."

Diana bolted upright in her chair. He registered the movement with intense satisfaction. His wife was awake. "What do you mean," she demanded slowly, *"not ready?"*

"I mean I'm not ready to sign."

"Why not?"

He lifted a shoulder, sloughing off the incredulous part of his mind that questioned his sanity. "I want more time."

Diana's eyes spit fire at him. "For what? You know I'm leaving the country in three weeks, Coburn. I want this done before that happens, and I'm sure you do, too."

He wasn't sure what he wanted anymore. But he was going to take his brother's advice and figure it out.

"So sorry to disturb your plans," he murmured in a voice as smooth as churned butter, "but that's just the way it is."

"Coburn." Jerry jumped in when it appeared his client might go loco. "It's highly unusual for a party to back out at this point when we have all the fine print agreed upon. Once Diana leaves the country, it's doubtful we can facilitate anything, given the spotty communications she might have where she is staying."

He gave the lawyer a withering look. "It took my wife twelve months to come out of hiding and face me. She can damn well wait for another few."

Jerry's jaw dropped. Chase gave Coburn a wary look as if appealing for direction. Diana flicked a look at the two lawyers, her eyes ice-cold and full of purpose. "Could you give us a second?"

The two men looked relieved to be leaving the room. Coburn closed the door with his foot behind them and stood watching his wife, arms folded over his chest. Diana got to her feet, crossed to him and stood mere inches away, her stony face not hiding for one moment what he could read in her eyes. "Don't you think last night was payback enough, Coburn? Why are you doing this?"

He narrowed his gaze on her. "You were the one to instigate the hot breakup sex this time, sweetheart. I only went along with it."

Fury wiped the composure from her face. "Do *not* do this to me. Do not play games with something so important."

"Why not?" He moved close enough to her that he could inhale her distinctive floral scent. Her fear. "How important was this to you when you ignored my phone calls for weeks? When you refused to talk it out like a rational human being?"

Her eyes flickered. "I did that because it was over. To end the vicious circle that happened between us time and time again… To *save* us."

"No." He caught her jaw in his fingers and commanded her attention. "You did it to save yourself. And to hell with how I felt."

"Coburn—"

"Save it." His razor-sharp words cut through the air like a knife. "Learn what it's like to wait and wonder, Diana. Learn what it's like to be stuck in purgatory like I was. I can tell you from experience it isn't pretty."

He turned and yanked open the door. Diana set a hand on his shoulder. "I am going. Jerry will find another way to make this happen, and it will be done. Do it the easy way without dragging us all through that."

He turned around, never feeling so cold and emotionless in his entire life. "Enjoy your self-exploration, Diana. I hope you get your answers."

He walked out of the conference room and away from the closure he'd wanted so desperately. If it added another complication to his already convoluted life? So be it. That had been far, far more satisfying than what he'd walked in there to do.

CHAPTER FOUR

"WHAT DO YOU MEAN, he wouldn't sign?"

Her father's enraged voice boomed in Diana's ear, intensifying the dull throb in her temples. She put down her spoon and pushed her half-eaten bowl of soup away as the ache in her head mixed with the uneasy sensation in her stomach to inspire a distinctly *unwell* feeling.

"He said he needed more time." She fixed her gaze on Wilbur Taylor's flinty, gray-eyed one and the expression he reserved solely for conversations about her ex-husband.

"More time for what?" her father huffed. "So he can add another socialite to his list of fame?"

Her mouth tightened. "I have no idea, and frankly I'm over it. I'm leaving on Friday. It can wait until he sees reason."

Her father waved a hand at her. "Never mind. I'll sic David Price on it."

She put her spoon down, her blood pressure rising. "Jerry is perfectly capable of taking care of it. It's my business, Father. Stay out of it."

"Jerry Simmons is a fine lawyer, but he isn't a pit bull like David. David will have you divorced in minutes."

"No." She cut the idea off at the pass. Although she couldn't say she didn't have her doubts about Jerry's ability to handle Coburn after her husband had walked all over him two weeks ago in that conference room, this was her decision to make, and she didn't want her father anywhere near it.

"Fine." Her father shrugged his broad shoulders. "But I don't think you're handling this very well. You shouldn't be giving him any choice."

Diana picked up her wine and took a sip. What *did* he think she handled well, beyond her patients? She'd spent her life trying to live up to her world-renowned orthopedic surgeon of a father, who overshadowed everything in his wake with his big personality and impossible standards. But measuring up had become a fruitless pursuit she'd finally abandoned for her own sanity.

"Your father is only considering what's best for you, Diana." Her mother, ever the peacekeeper, attempted to smooth the waters.

And pursuing his own witch hunt of her husband… Her father had never liked Coburn from the minute he'd laid eyes on him. She'd always wondered if it was because he saw too much of himself in Coburn—a man who viewed the world as his oyster and took his pick of it as if it was his divine right. That was what her father had done in marrying her mother, his secretary at the time, then carrying on a five-year-long affair with a brilliant fellow doctor whose brain apparently turned him on more than his society wife.

At least Coburn had never cheated on her. She sat back as the maid came to clear her soup bowl. He'd waited until they'd ended their marriage to drink his fill. Which satisfied his code of honor. As long as he was in a relationship, he never strayed, even if, as Rory had joked to her about his friend's philandering ways when they'd first met, it was only one night. Not once during their turbulent union had he ever indicated interest in another woman, despite the way they'd shamelessly thrown themselves at him.

It should have quieted her insecurities, but they'd been far too deeply ingrained to elude.

Her mother scrunched up her angularly attractive face. "I don't like the idea of you over there in that *wild* country, Diana. Anything could happen to you and we are so far away. I wish you'd reconsider."

"I am needed there." She gave her mother a pained look. "We've been over this."

"The situation was never this bad," her father broke in, a bullish look on his face. "Yes, the city is more stable now, but the rebels have still been conducting raids, and conditions could deteriorate overnight."

Diana was well aware of the situation she was walking into. She'd come to terms with the danger when she'd made the decision to commit. And although her nerves were growing every day at the thought of what she was about to face—a mental and physical challenge that would surely change her life—she was determined to follow through.

"I'm not changing my mind."

"I rather thought so." Her father grimaced at her from across the solid, ornately carved mahogany table. "So I reached out to a contact of mine there and arranged for you to stay in the Lione Hotel instead of the usual accommodations. It's minutes to the hospital and has the best security you can hope for right now. Someone will walk you back and forth each day."

Diana stared at him in disbelief as the maid set the steaming main course down in front of her. "*Dammit*, Father, this is my life. You can't just do things like that."

"I wouldn't have to if you weren't being so foolhardy."

"Part of this experience is bonding with the other doctors I'm working with. I want to stay with them."

"There is another doctor staying at the Lione. Bond with him."

She gave him an exasperated look. "You have to stop interfering in my life."

Her father picked up his fork and pointed it at her. "Do

you know how many foreign-aid workers have been kidnapped from that area in the past six months? It is *staggering*, Diana. If you won't do this for yourself, do it for your mother and me so we don't spend every day and night worrying about you."

Worrying about your half-a-million-dollar investment in your only child, she corrected flippantly to herself. But the real hint of concern in her father's voice made her soften. It wasn't fair to make them worry.

"Fine." She picked up her fork and matched his aggressive joust with one of her own. "But *do not* make *one* more phone call, *one* more inquiry on my behalf to anyone, or I will stay with the others."

"Fine." Her father dug into his beef with a satisfied nod. Diana looked down at hers, her stomach doing a slow roll at the smell of the spicy dish. She cut a piece of the meat. A wave of perspiration swept over her, blanketing her forehead in a thin layer of sweat.

Oh, no. Bile rose in her throat. She swallowed it back down, pushed her chair out and ran for the bathroom. She barely made it inside and to the toilet before she was brutally, gut-wrenchingly sick. Her insides heaving until there was nothing left inside her, she remained kneeling on the bathroom floor draped over the toilet until finally, her head stopped spinning and she could sit up.

What bloody bad timing. She grabbed some toilet paper and wiped it over her brow. She never got sick, never got the flu. Coburn used to call her stomach cast-iron, which made it all the more ironic her succumbing to it now with days to go before she had to get on a plane for a multiday trip.

Deciding she was in the safe zone, she got to her feet and washed her hands. The fact that this was the third day in a row she'd suffered a low-grade and now acute nausea penetrated her consciousness. Her uninhibited encounter with Coburn filled her head.

They'd used a condom. They'd always used condoms because she couldn't tolerate the birth control pill and the last thing she and Coburn had needed was a baby at this point in their careers. To complicate their marriage.

It must be the flu.

She went back to the dining room, where her parents insisted she stay the night. But a sixth sense told her she couldn't be here right now. She asked them to call her a cab instead and went home, where Beth fussed over her and made her a cup of tea, then put her to bed.

She tried to sleep but her head was spinning as if a circus was going on inside it. What if it wasn't the flu? What if she was pregnant?

A giant knot formed in her stomach. She stared out the window at the big oak tree swaying back and forth in the darkness, high winds signaling the imminent arrival of a classic East Coast electrical storm. If she'd thought what had happened upon seeing her ex again had been a disaster, that was nothing compared with the possibilities raging through her head. *Nothing.*

She spent two days in denial. On the third, she had a scheduled appointment with her doctor to receive a final shot she needed for her trip. Joanne Gibson, her GP and a former colleague, gave her a frown as she entered the examining room.

"You look thin. Have you been ill?"

Diana sat down in a chair, the tiny room seeming to close in on her at the question. "Could you add a—" she could barely get the words out "—pregnancy test to the list?"

Joanne's face lit up. "Really? Are you and Coburn back to—?" The look on Diana's face stopped her cold. "What a stupid thing to say," her doctor mumbled. "Of course we can do that."

They did the pregnancy test first because Joanne wanted to make sure the shot she was giving her was fine if she was pregnant. Diana stared at the wall, examining the cracks in the plaster until she'd memorized every last one. She could not be pregnant. This could not be happening to her now, not when she was about to walk away from everything she knew. It could not.

Joanne came back a short while later, a studied blank look on her face. Diana's heart seized in her chest. She knew that look. It was the one she used when she had tricky news to give to a patient.

"You are pregnant," her doctor confirmed quietly. "I take it this was unexpected?"

Disastrous. *Untenable* was more like it. She wanted to be happy. She wanted to be a mother. Hell, she wanted to be a pediatric surgeon. Of course she wanted kids. *But now? With Coburn?* A haze of unreality spread over her that was so thick, so unnavigable, she couldn't claw her way through it.

"There are options, you know."

"No." She barked the word out. *That* was not an option. Ever.

"Okay. I'd like to examine you, then. Just to make sure everything is okay. And since you have a rare blood condition in your family, I'd like to take some tests for that."

Diana nodded. She somehow made her way through the next half hour without screaming, without losing her composure as Joanne examined her, because she was too numb to feel anything. This was supposed to be *her* time. *Her* chance at a new life. And she had messed it up royally over her lust for a man who had already wreaked havoc on her life for long enough.

Oh. My. God.

Joanne sent her off with a promise to deliver the test results in a few days. Diana found herself in the park across the street with a cup of peppermint tea in her hand, sitting on a bench while she watched the dark crimson and orange leaves fall off the trees as fall set in. It was just enough normalcy to convince her she hadn't entered some alternate universe where condoms failed on the one night you had sex with your ex whom you were now tied to for at least the next two decades.

Anger spread through her, slowly overtaking the numbness. *How could this happen?* Because it was clearly *her* problem. Coburn had washed his hands of her that night at his place, had made it clear she meant nothing to him. He would support this baby, no doubt; he was that kind of a man. But if she could have dreamed up the worst possible scenario of *anything* and thrown it at her husband, it would not have made Coburn any greener than the thought of a baby.

Her stomach lurched, protesting even the tea. She set the cup down and breathed in through her nose. Her husband hadn't even been capable of *talking* about a baby when she'd broached the subject casually to test the waters because she'd known someday it was in the cards for her. Whether it had something to do with his tumultuous, on-again, off-again relationship with his brother, Harrison, or his aloof family upbringing, she wasn't sure. She'd just gotten the message loud and clear it wasn't on his agenda.

That awful scene in the boardroom when they'd been allocating the pieces from their life together as if their marriage was a board game ran through her head. A bubble of hysterical laughter formed in her throat. What would have happened if she'd thrown a baby into the mix? Her husband had been halfway off the ledge without such a mind-numbing complication as their flesh and blood being tied together for eternity.

She sat on the bench as the bright midday sunshine faded to late afternoon, trying to absorb the enormity of the news she'd been given. The spontaneity, the freedom she'd craved to spread her wings, was about to be taken from her by the little person growing inside her. Her life as she knew it was about to change irrevocably.

Panic clawed at her throat, a terror she had never known before it reached up to steal her breath. Was she supposed to tell Coburn and have him insist she not go to Africa, which she knew he'd do? Or did she go, knowing there was no medical reason why she shouldn't? First trimesters were uneventful, as Joanne had said. She was perfectly healthy and strong. She could scrap her plan to go for a year and simply execute her initial contract.

Her thoughts slowed, her breathing calming as her decision cemented itself. When she looked up to see the sky darkening over the park, purple streaks lacing a hazy gray sky, she got up, tossed her cup into the garbage can and flagged a cab. At home, she finished packing and closed off all the loose ends of her life. Except for the biggest one of them all.

Two days later, she stepped on a plane bound for London, where she would stay overnight with a friend, then continue on to Africa. Her mind was resolute and focused. She was grabbing her dream with both hands. *Then* she would call Coburn when she was settled and give him the news that would undoubtedly rock his world. She liked the idea of having a continent between them when that happened. It seemed so much less confrontational.

CHAPTER FIVE

COBURN HAD JUST left a meeting in midtown and was standing on the street, an espresso and his briefcase in one hand while he unlocked the door of his Jaguar with the other, when his mobile rang.

It never stopped ringing these days. He had a newfound respect for Harrison spending that many years under siege as CEO with every matter of crisis or political ripple that seemed to run through the company at regular intervals.

Cursing as the phone pealed again, he set his espresso down on the roof of the car, dropped his briefcase and pulled his phone out of his pocket. Dr. Joanne Gibson, said the caller ID. *Who?* He filed through his brain. *Diana's doctor.* Why would she be calling him? He almost ignored it, then remembered he was listed as an emergency contact for his wife.

"Coburn here."

"Coburn?" The voice sounded confused. "Oh, hi. Sorry, Mr. Grant, Rebecca from Joanne Gibson's office here. I was trying to reach Diana. Your number's listed right below hers."

"No worries. You might have trouble getting her, though. She's out of the country as of today."

"I thought I might catch her before she left. *Has* she left?"

"I wouldn't know," he said pleasantly.

A pause. "Oh. Okay. I have some test results I need to give to her. Do you know if she took her usual mobile with her or if she's switching over?"

"I wouldn't know that, either." He started to mutter a polite kiss-off, then frowned and tucked the phone closer to his ear. "What test?"

"I can't really say. It's just a routine check with her preg—" The woman broke off as someone said something to her in the background. "Just a routine test," she repeated. "I'm sorry to have bothered you."

His blood ran cold. "Just one second," he ordered. "Were you about to say *pregnancy*? Is my wife *pregnant*?"

"I'm sorry, Mr. Grant, I really can't tell you—"

"Put Dr. Gibson on the phone."

"What? I can't do that. She's with a patient."

"Then, unpatient her *now* or I will get in my car, drive over there and do it myself."

A pause. "Just one minute."

He drummed his fingers on the midnight blue paint of his car, a complete sense of unreality enveloping him as he digested what he knew the receptionist had been about to say. This could not be happening. He'd worn a condom that night. He'd very definitely worn a condom that night. But condoms weren't foolproof…

Cars whizzed by him, the height of Manhattan rush-hour traffic jamming itself onto the streets. The voice of an older female finally came on the line. "Coburn?"

"Yes," he said tersely. "Your receptionist just called me by mistake, as I'm sure she told you, and mentioned in passing my wife is pregnant. *My wife* who is now on a plane bound for *Africa*. Could you confirm this rather important piece of information?"

"Coburn…" He heard the hesitation in her voice. "Rebecca should not have given that information out. It breaches doctor-patient confidentiality laws."

"I understand that. But since the cat's out of the bag, I suggest you confirm it right now so I don't have to spend all my money *suing you* for the information."

Joanne sighed. "I am so sorry this happened. I truly am. But Diana really needs to be the one to tell you this."

He held the phone away from his ear and stared at it as if it was a toy he would like to crush. Rage zigzagged through him, singeing his skin. She had just told him everything he needed to know.

"You know what, Dr. Gibson?" he bit out, pulling the phone back to his ear. "Forget it."

He disconnected the call, picked up his briefcase, tossed it into the car and headed uptown to Diana's parents' place. He was two blocks into the journey before he remembered he'd left his espresso on the roof of the car. An expletive flew from his lips. He wasn't a violent man, but the urge to slowly strangle his wife was profound.

Traffic was filthy. He spent the first fifteen minutes crawling at a snail's pace behind cabs that wove in and out of his lane, not helping his temper. By the time he got stuck a few blocks from the Taylors' penthouse, his head was in total disarray. He leaned back against the seat and attempted to take it all in. Could Diana have been pregnant the night she'd been with him? Was it someone else's baby? The shattered look on her face after he'd taken her that night sliced through his head. No way. There was *no way* she was dating someone else and had been with him like that. He knew his wife. It wasn't in her DNA. Which left him with the mind-numbing conclusion that this baby was his. He was going to be a father.

And his wife was on her way to *Africa*. To an unstable city in the interior that had just come out of a period of dangerous unrest. And she had *known* she was pregnant. *Known* she was carrying his child.

By the time he'd crawled the last couple of blocks to the Taylors' building, he knew one thing. He wasn't waiting around for Diana to deign to tell him the news. She had taken a liberty with information, information about his child. Action was required.

The doorman of the Taylors' building caught the keys he threw at him as he swept past without breaking stride. Barking his name at the concierge, he fixed the man with an unrelenting stare until he put the phone down and waved him through. *Be civil*, he told himself while stalking toward the elevator. This was not the Taylors' fault; it was their daughter's. He was here only to get the information he needed.

The elevator stopped at the Taylors' tenth-floor penthouse. Wilbur Taylor opened the door seconds after he rapped on it, *hard*.

"Coburn," the other man murmured smoothly. "What an unexpected surprise."

"You can dispense with the pleasantries," Coburn suggested tersely, walking past him into the foyer. "We all know how much you like me."

Wilbur blinked at the open aggression Coburn usually managed to hide beneath a cloak of civility. Diana's father closed the door and faced him, a light firing in his eyes at the opportunity to take the gloves off. "I'd like you more if you gave my daughter the divorce she's asking for."

"That might be wishful thinking, since she's pregnant with my child."

Wilbur's jaw dropped. Diana's mother, who had appeared behind her husband, immaculately dressed in pants and a sweater, went chalk white. *"Pregnant?"*

He was heartened to see it hadn't been a conspiracy against him. "You didn't know?"

Her mother shook her head. "She wasn't well when she

was here for dinner on Sunday but we thought it was the flu." She shook her head, her blue eyes flickering. "She left knowing that?"

"The height of stupidity, don't you think?"

"Now, listen," Wilbur interjected, "You can't talk—"

"I *can*," Coburn raged, pointing a finger at him. "Right now I am capable of *anything* given what your daughter has done. But all I want from you is the address where she's staying."

Wilbur gave him a long look. "You're going to bring her back."

"Damn right I am."

A long silence wrapped itself around the three of them. Wilbur scratched his head. "This may be the only time we'll ever agree on anything, Grant."

Coburn cocked a brow at him. "The address?"

"She's staying at the Lione Hotel in the capital."

He promised to update Diana's parents when he could and left.

At home, a glass of Scotch in his hand to numb the furor in his head, he called Frankie and told her to clear his schedule for the next week. If she thought this strange given his jam-packed slate of important meetings, she didn't comment. Next he called his pilot and had him file a flight plan for the day after next—his destination, the large, landlocked nation in the center of Africa his wife was headed to.

He dropped onto the sofa, tipped his head back and swallowed a mouthful of the Scotch, welcoming its fiery burn as it warmed his insides. Diana clearly had an idea of how she thought this was going to play out. Unfortunately for her, that wasn't going to happen. He'd had more than enough time to think while gridlocked in Manhattan traffic, and he knew exactly how *his* version of events was going to unfold. It had nothing to do with choices or selfishness and everything to do with repercussions. *Responsibility.*

He refilled his Scotch and took it out onto the terrace with him. A rare smattering of stars dotted the New York sky. He studied them, wondering exactly how far away they were. How many light-years from his own life were they? How many light-years had his life moved today?

It had changed irrevocably with one piece of earth-shattering news. He'd always known Diana wanted children, knew he likely didn't, but had reserved judgment for the moment he had to make that decision. And now that choice had been taken out of his hands.

The combustible way he and Diana had come together here that night three weeks ago filled his head. The premonition that making love to her in his bed was a road he couldn't return from. His mouth twisted. How right he'd been. He was going to be a father. He was now tied to the woman he'd vowed to forget. His intuition had been telling him something and he had not listened.

A low curse split his lips as he looked up into the night sky. He supposed his reluctance to be a father stemmed from his need to not be tied down. To preserve his freedom at all costs. The dysfunctional nature of his own family. But presented with the facts, he was surprised to discover absolute clarity that stemmed from someplace deep inside him. Maybe it was biology, maybe it was because this baby was his flesh and blood, but he knew that no matter how bad the timing, no matter what state his dismal marriage was in, this was a responsibility he could not shirk. He and Diana were going to have to make this work.

A knot formed in his stomach. His wife had taken a piece of him with her when she'd walked out of their apartment that night, proclaiming what they had dead. Now she was about to learn what it was like to be bound to a person forever with no hope for the future. Because that was *his* plan.

CHAPTER SIX

IT WAS STILL smoking hot at eight o'clock at night as the sun sank behind the skyline of the central African capital Diana had been posted to, blazing a fiery path as it scorched everything within its reach. She put up a hand to shield her eyes as she left the hospital with her armed escort after her second day of work and walked the short distance to her hotel. She was normally good with heat, loved it in fact, but since she'd arrived here, the heat wave that had racked the country had been beyond anything she'd ever experienced. Sweltering and bone-dry, it invaded every cell, sucking out all your bodily fluids along with it.

Which would have been manageable if she hadn't been pregnant and losing hydration to the ever-present nausea that continued to plague her. The work had been even more emotionally draining and physically taxing than she'd imagined. She'd been posted here to treat patients at the hospital and clinic who had been directly or indirectly injured in the violence between the rebels and the armed self-defense groups battling over the city. Although the arrival of international forces had stemmed the violence for now, there were still random acts of aggression taking place on civilians, and the fallout from the hostilities had provided a steady stream of patients through the hospital doors.

She had performed surgery today on a sixty-year-old man who'd stumbled upon a grenade that hadn't been defused and almost lost a leg, done a cesarean section on a young mother and helped the other doctors work through dozens of patients suffering from everything from malaria to respiratory and skin infections. All of it had been performed in an emergency room that lacked much of the high-tech equipment she was used to, requiring instinct and ingenuity on her part to make do.

She knew what she'd seen today would haunt her for a lifetime. And that was just *one day* in the life of this besieged city. It was enough to break your heart, something her supervisor had counseled her about. "You need to keep your professional detachment," he'd told her. "Even more so than you would normally do. You are going to see things here that will affect your perspective forever. Which will test your belief in your fellow man. You've got to move past it."

The gleaming facade of the Lione Hotel loomed in front of them, sparkling a burned-gold color in the dying rays of the sun. She smiled her thanks to her escort and arranged to meet him the next morning. If it seemed incongruous for a five-star hotel to still be operating in this city after what it had endured, it should be noted things weren't working entirely as usual.

There still wasn't hot water when she went to take a shower in her lovely whitewashed room with its four-poster bed, nor was the AC working particularly well. Wanting only to drink and sleep, but knowing she had to eat for the sake of the new life growing inside her, Diana went down to the restaurant and ordered a light dinner. She managed to eat her salad and half the chicken before she gave up and took her tea out onto the terrace, which seemed to be cooler than the poorly air-conditioned restaurant.

At least the air *moved* out here, she thought, sinking into a chair at a table by the pool.

The terrace was deserted except for a man leaning

against the facade of the restaurant smoking a cigarette. She focused her gaze on the smooth surface of the oval-shaped pool, a jewel in the center of the perfectly landscaped space. It looked heavenly. Almost good enough to inspire a trip to her room to get her bathing suit, but even that was too much energy in her current state. She sank back in the chair and looked up at the dusky sky and the different placement of the stars on this side of the world.

The man dropped the butt of his cigarette to the concrete, ground it under his foot and went back inside. The night blanketed her in silence. Her eyes fluttered shut. Exhaustion reached out to claim her with greedy, grasping hands. She wasn't sure how much time had passed, three, four minutes, when a sixth sense made her open her eyes. A man strolled from the shadows of the building, dressed all in black. A bolt of alarm zigzagged through her, penetrating the fog she was in. *Move*, her brain told her. But by the time she got to her feet, her hands balled at her sides ready to engage, the tall figure had stepped into the light, not ten feet from her.

Her eyes widened. It was not an unknown assailant. It was someone much more dangerous.

"Coburn." The word came out half croak, her eyes moving over his tall, lean body clad in black jeans and a black T-shirt. "What are you doing here?"

He stepped fully into the light, moving lithely, catlike, toward her until he was so close she could see the ominous glitter in his beautiful blue eyes. A shiver went down her spine. She was in trouble. So much trouble.

His gaze locked onto hers. "When were you going to tell me, Diana? How long did you deem it acceptable to keep from me that I'm going to be a father?"

Her heart leaped into her mouth. He knew. Of course he knew. He was *here*. She pushed a breath past her locked set of lungs. "How did you find out?"

"Your doctor's office called looking for you. Apparently the new receptionist hasn't yet learned the ropes because she let your big secret slip."

Oh, God. Her knees went weak at the thought of how angry he must have been. Still was…

"And the hotel?" she asked weakly. "How did you find out I was here?"

"Your father. He was more than happy to address this insane behavior of yours."

Her heart dropped. "You told him about the baby."

His mouth compressed into a straight, forbidding line. "I did what I needed to do. And believe me, they were just as shocked as I was that you would travel halfway across the world pregnant and suffering from morning sickness to take up a physically grueling position you *know* you shouldn't be doing."

Her shoulders shot to her ears. "I don't *know* anything of the kind. There is absolutely no reason why I, a perfectly healthy woman in my first trimester, shouldn't be here."

"No *reason*?" he repeated, the glint in his eyes turning positively flammable. "I stopped at the hospital and met with your supervisor. He had no idea you were pregnant. He said you'd been sick on the job yesterday and he'd been concerned but had put it down to first-day jitters."

Her jaw dropped open. "You *talked* to my supervisor?"

"Didn't you just hear me, Diana?" His lips curved in a savage twist. "I will do whatever it takes to make you see sense since you obviously can't do it for yourself."

Which meant what? Fury at the boundaries he'd crossed mixed with fear to render her speechless. Her gaze flicked over the clenched muscles of his jaw, the tendons and veins that stood out in stark relief against the strong column of his throat. Anger seemed to vibrate from every pore of him. He was beyond furious with her.

"Congratulations," he rasped, reading her expression.

"You have successfully diagnosed my current mood. Now *answer the question, Diana*. When were you going to tell me? After you had this all figured out in that structured brain of yours? After you'd worked out how we divide our paternal rights? Exactly how you want this to play out... What *roles* you'd like me to assume in our child's life?" A dangerous glitter stoked his gaze. "Because I can assure you, after this stunt, it has *backfired* on you."

The breath whooshed from her lungs. "Coburn, I needed time to think, time to process. You can't blame me for that."

"No," he agreed tightly. "I can't. What I *can* be livid about is you waltzing off to take this assignment when you *knew* you were carrying our baby. *Without telling me*." He shook his head, a vicious expression darkening his eyes. "I knew you were selfish, but *this*, this was unforgivable."

Her heart thudded in her chest. "I was going to tell you this week as soon as I got settled."

"Instead, I found out from a receptionist I was going to be a father. A *receptionist*. While I was getting into my car on the corner of Fifth and Fourteenth to be precise." He stepped closer, until she could feel the fury emanating from him. "You were afraid I would have made you cancel your trip if you'd told me."

Her jaw dipped. He slid his fingers beneath it and brought her gaze back up to his. "Unbelievable. You are *unbelievable*."

She pulled out of his grip. "I am exercising my right to be an independent human being. I was planning on consulting you with this pregnancy every step of the way."

His mouth tightened. "Unfortunately for you, the time for consultation and negotiation is over. You gave away that right the moment you elected to leave the country without coming to me."

The ice in his tone spoke a dire warning. She swallowed

hard as it slid through her, chilling her despite the sweltering air. "You are upset," she reasoned, laying a hand on his arm in an attempt to redirect the storm. "I agree I shouldn't have left without telling you. Let's sit down and talk about it."

He looked down at her hand on his arm as if it were a pest he wanted to stomp under his feet. "No more talking. We play by my rules now."

Her heart skipped a beat. "What does that mean?"

"It means you have ten minutes to pack your things before we leave. The jet is waiting at the airport."

Her breath snagged in her throat. She shook her head and backed away. "I am not coming with you. I have a contract to fulfill."

"Not anymore, you don't. Your supervisor agrees the best thing to do is to send you home and bring you back another time."

Her dream vaporized before her eyes. She took another step backward, her head moving from side to side. "No, Coburn."

He stalked forward, his hand reaching out to snag her forearm as she wobbled backward, nearly taking a fully clothed dip in the pool. Desperation surged through her as her fingers closed around his waist, her gaze rising to his ice-cold blue one. "Don't do this."

"It's already done."

Helplessness plunged through her. "In nine months I'm having this baby, and once that happens I won't be able to do anything for years. This is *my time*, Coburn." She punctuated the words with the slap of her palm to his chest. "I won't let you take it away from me."

He looked down at her palm pushing ineffectually against his chest. As if she was a juvenile in need of restraint. "Pull yourself together," he advised coldly, lifting his gaze to her face. "You have your entire life to do this. Just not now."

She gritted her teeth. She wanted to tell him his outrageous arrogance wasn't winning this time. That he couldn't tell her what to do, not any longer. But a tiny part of her, a part she'd been ignoring ever since she'd arrived here and seen the physical challenges she'd face if this nausea went on, which it might for another few weeks, had already been questioning the wisdom of her decision. Was *scared.*

Did she need to accept that Coburn was right? That the timing was the timing and she was powerless to fight it except with the knowledge that she *would* come back. She *would* do this.

A tear slid down her face. Then another. She lifted her fingers to brush them away, but the hot drops of desperation kept rolling like runaway bandits down her cheeks. Once, just once, she'd wanted to do something for herself. Something to bring her soul back from the depths it had sunk to.

Coburn reached up and brushed her fingers aside, sweeping the tears away with his thumbs. The hard glint in his eyes softened a fraction. "This is not over," he said quietly. "It's just postponed."

"And what's been postponed for you?" she asked bitterly. "You are a CEO. You have the ultimate power. You don't even *want* a baby. You want to control me. *This.*"

His mouth tightened. "I never said I didn't want a baby."

"Your complete avoidance of the subject said it for you. Every time I tried to talk it through so we were on the same page, you said it was a future conversation."

"It *was* a future conversation. The timing wasn't right for either of us. But regardless of how I feel on the matter, the fact is, we *are* pregnant. We need to deal with it, and running away and hiding isn't going to work."

"I wasn't running away. This was planned."

"*Before* you added our baby's health to the equation."

She studied the taut, sharply defined lines of his face. This was a Coburn she didn't know. The tough, impenetrable iteration of him that had emerged from their bitter split.

A total stranger.

"Show me where your room is," he ordered. "We have one shot to get out of here tonight, and I'm not missing it."

Her shoulders slumped, exhaustion taking her in one fell swoop. She didn't have the energy to lift another finger, let alone go through another day like the one she'd just had.

She lifted her gaze to his. "I will come with you because I agree it's the right thing to do. But you will not order me around, Coburn. Not anymore."

His rock-hard expression didn't change. "Let's go."

She led him into the hotel and upstairs to her room. She didn't have much to pack because she'd brought only the bare essentials. They checked out and traveled to the airport in a dark sedan with blacked-out windows manned by two big burly security types.

With an ease only the Grant family's connections could produce, they were ushered through a quick separate security check and onto the company jet. Diana buckled into her seat and watched her dream fly out the window as the plane took off, banking over the sprawling capital city and heading west. So angry with Coburn, so angry at everything, she laid her head back against the cushiony seat as soon as they were airborne and closed her eyes.

She fell asleep almost instantly in the seductive coolness of the perfectly climate-controlled jet. She woke halfway through their journey as they refueled in Spain, ate the omelet the flight attendant served once they were airborne and went back to sleep. She must have slept for a long, long time, because when she woke again it was dark and Coburn was nudging her to put her seat belt on for landing.

She rubbed her eyes, drunk on sleep, and slid the belt

on. Looking out the window, she searched for the bright lights of New York. It was pitch-black outside. She looked at Coburn, confused. "Didn't you say we were about to land?"

He looked up from his paperwork. "We are."

She looked out the window again. It was as if they were in the middle of nowhere. Alarm bells rocketed through her. *"Where are we?"*

"About twenty miles north of an island in the Caribbean."

Her vision went red. "You said you were taking me home."

"Eventually, yes, I will."

Her fingernails dug into the leather seat rest at the nonchalant expression on his face. "What do you mean, *eventually*?"

He looked at her then, an expression of deadly intent in his eyes. "I've taken a week off work. My friend Arthur Kent has offered us the guest cottage on his private island."

"Why?" The question was delivered in a tone just short of shrill.

"Because," he drawled, "you and I are about to put our marriage back together for the sake of this baby, Diana. It's just you, me, this island and a whole lot of soul-searching to do."

Her breath jammed in her throat. "You can't be serious."

He sat back in his chair and folded his arms across his chest. "I've never been so serious about anything in my life."

That night at his apartment flashed through her head. The extreme destruction they had wreaked together... How it'd felt as if he'd gutted her as a hunter did a prime piece of kill...

She shook her head. "It will never work. Nothing about us works anymore, Coburn."

An emotion she couldn't read flickered in his eyes. "I

think we proved in *creating* this disaster that some things still do work."

Heat stained her cheeks. "Sexual compatibility does not make a relationship."

"But it is an integral part of it." He moved his gaze over her face, raked it down over her body in a blatant perusal, then brought it back up again. "If we have to build some kind of a foundation on my ability to make you beg, so be it. We aren't leaving this island until we learn how to communicate, sweetheart. If *getting you off* gets me into your head, I won't hesitate to play that card."

Her nails dug harder into the leather. She had both hands on her seat belt ready to pounce on him when the attendant came into the cabin to check they were buckled up. She fell back into her seat, temples pounding.

Coburn's gaze glittered. "Hang on to that emotion a little longer, tiger. We're alone on the island until Thursday night. Soon you can let it all out."

As if. She pressed her lips together mutinously. She might be having a baby with him, but she was not spending the week on a deserted island trying to put their marriage back together. *Or sleeping with him again.* Definitely not that.

The first thing she was going to do when they stepped off the plane and she was alone was call her father and get him to charter a plane to come get her.

Except it was the middle of the night when they touched down on the runway. A waiting car and driver drove them to a dock on the edge of the palm tree-strewn island, and there they transferred to a boat. She took in the inky dark sea that loomed around them as they zoomed across it toward a tiny island ahead that glimmered with a handful of lights.

They *were* in the middle of nowhere. Literally. Panic settled into her bones, deep and jarring.

When they reached the shore, she stepped out into the steamy night air that carried the scent of a dozen tropical flowers and the salt of the sea. There was only a canopy of palm trees fronting a lush forest. She couldn't see anything beyond.

Coburn ushered her into the Jeep SUV waiting for them, then slid in beside her. The road they traveled was a narrow, bumpy passageway. She closed her eyes against the nausea that rose in her throat from too much motion. Too much emotion. Fatigue overtook her again. She fought it, but it'd been as if she'd had a sleeping sickness since she'd gotten pregnant, and she hadn't slept well in Africa.

"Sleep," Coburn instructed beside her. "We've got a good twenty-minute ride across the island."

More to avoid him, she rested her head back against the seat and let her eyes close. She would call her father in the morning. Then the cavalry would be on its way.

CHAPTER SEVEN

DIANA AWOKE TO brilliant sunshine, a pure, magnetic version of it that reflected off the turquoise sea in a blinding display of light that cast everything in a warm, resonant glow. She would have lain there, reveling in it, had the thought of exactly where she was not flashed through her head at that precise moment. And whom she was with.

A fuzzy memory of Coburn carrying her in from the car, half-asleep, and up to this room followed it. She had woken only long enough to ensure herself he was sleeping somewhere else before she'd buried her face in the lavender-scented sheets and surrendered again to unconsciousness.

She flicked her gaze to the door. She needed to get out of here.

Swinging her legs over the side of the bed, she reached for the short robe draped over the back of a chair and pulled it on. With barely a glance at the beautiful nautically themed room with its huge canopied four-poster bed and multiple views across the sparkling sea, she found her purse on a chair near the window and rummaged through it for her phone. Rummaged some more. Frowned. She had definitely put it in there when they'd left Africa. It was the one thing she wouldn't leave behind.

Coburn. Heat, the combustible kind, spread through her like wildfire. Yanking the door to her room open, she flew down the hallway to the other bedrooms in search of her target. But they were all empty, including the one Coburn had commandeered. Spinning around, she left the room and went down the stairs two by two to the living room. The beautiful airy space that overlooked the sea was empty. So was the magnificent library with its ten-foot-high built-in bookcases and scads of priceless old volumes lining them. She turned on her heel and walked toward the kitchen, the only place she hadn't checked. It was empty, too. If she knew Coburn, he was out for a ten-mile jog or taming the water with some sort of boat or machine.

Combing the kitchen, she searched for a phone. When she didn't find one there she went back to the library. It didn't have one, either. What kind of a house didn't have phones? Had Coburn gotten rid of them along with her cell phone?

Her heart slammed into her chest. She could not be kidnapped on a private island. She could *not*. She spied Coburn's laptop on the desk. Pouncing on it, she tried to log on, but it was password protected. A curse escaped her lips. *Really?*

She went back to the kitchen, looking for something, *anything* that would tell her where she was. She was rifling through drawers when Coburn strolled lazily into the kitchen in shorts and a T-shirt soaked with perspiration. She froze, hand in the drawer.

"Looking for something?"

She pulled her hand out of the drawer, closed it and leaned against the counter. "My phone, actually. You wouldn't happen to know where it is?"

"I took it," he responded casually. Conversationally. "You can't have it."

Her blood boiled in her veins. She pushed away from the counter and crossed the kitchen to stand in front of him, her body vibrating with fury. "Give me my phone."

"No. We are here to work through our issues, Diana. I'll not have you calling Daddy so you can orchestrate a rescue."

"That would be difficult when I don't know where I am."

"Double insurance."

She looked at him in disbelief. "You can't keep me here like this. Kidnapping is a crime."

His mouth curved. "You are my wife. That would be kind of hard to prove." He waved a hand at her as if she was a six-year-old in need of diversion. "Why don't you go put on a bathing suit and come for a swim? The sea's like bathwater."

Her boiling blood heated to a ferocious roll. He was holding her here against her will, had taken her phone and now he wanted her to go swimming with him? Was he insane? She flew at him, her fingernails poised to inflict maximum damage. He caught her easily, his fingers manacling around her forearms. "I take it that's a no?"

She struggled against his grip. "You can't do this. Let me call my father right now and I will consider giving you partial custody of this child by not siccing the police on you for kidnapping."

He tightened his fingers around her wrists, his blue gaze ice-cold as it rested on her face. "You left me no choice, Di. You walked away from me without telling me we were having a baby. If I take you back to New York you will disappear again and I will be talking to you through our lawyers. And since I intend for us to make this marriage work for the sake of our child, that is not happening. We are hashing this out right now, this inability to coexist together."

"In a *week*? I understand you are angry. I understand we have things to work out with regards to this baby, but I am *not* staying married to you, Coburn."

"Why?" His gaze lashed her face, all belligerent testosterone. "Don't you think it's better for our baby to grow up with both parents?"

"If we didn't *hate* each other, yes."

His gaze narrowed. "We have a lot of emotions in the mix right now, but hatred isn't one of them."

She wasn't sure what to call it, but whatever it was, it wasn't a good basis for a marriage. "We can't make this work. We've proved that."

"The only thing we've *proved* is what doesn't work. How good we are at running away from our problems instead of facing them."

Her eyes widened. "Yes," he said harshly, "I'm including myself in that. I know I wasn't perfect, either. We have fundamentally different views on how we want to live our lives, Diana, but somehow we are going to have to reconcile those views for the sake of this baby. To give him or her a chance to grow up with the solid foundation of a cohesive family unit."

"What if I want to be happy?" she blurted out. "You don't want to marry anyone else right now, but what if you do someday? What if I want to? Shouldn't I have that choice?"

His eyes darkened into that midnight shade of blue she knew signaled imminent danger. "You don't want to marry someone else, Di, because if you did, you would have filed for divorce months ago. You wouldn't have waited a year to do it, until you were about to step on a plane and fly off to another continent so the coward in you wouldn't have to face your unresolved feelings for me until the papers were signed and we were beyond the point of no return."

"I don't have unresolved feelings for you."

His mouth twisted in a derisive curl. "That night on my terrace was strictly you getting yourself off, was it? The questions you asked about my other women, the way you tried to take me apart? That was all because you are so over me. I can see it now."

An all-over body flush suffused her. "That was closure for me, Coburn."

"Yeah, you looked like you had it when you left." He studied her with that analytical intensity that seemed to reach right inside her. "There's this thing that happens when I touch you. A need inside of you to connect that makes you slip out of that shell of yours and try to crawl inside of me. I can *feel* it when you do it. I felt it that night we were together, Diana. It's still there."

The husky play of his words singed her skin. If she'd tried to verbalize how being with Coburn made her feel, she couldn't have done it better. Except he didn't want her anymore—he wanted his child.

"I think you flatter yourself," she denied. "Are you sure that isn't your own emotion talking? Because there was a hell of a lot of anger in you that night, Coburn."

"There still is." He surprised her by admitting it. "But we're talking about you and your refusal to acknowledge your emotions. You ran away because I was forcing you to address a part of yourself that terrifies you. You were afraid I would break down those walls and leave you wide-open for scrutiny."

"That's ridiculous," she scoffed, pulling against his hold. "Let me go."

"Not until you admit it."

"Admit what?"

"You still have feelings for me we can build on."

"I *don't*." She lifted her chin. "But even if I did, why would I tell you, a man who professes to feel nothing for me?"

A guarded expression passed over his face. "I believe if we put the past behind us, we can find something in what we had. Maybe it won't be love, but it can be *enough*."

A sharp pain went through her at his blunt admission. "You honestly think that's enough to raise a child together?"

"I *know* it is. It's more than the political arrangement my parents had. They didn't even sleep together. There was no affection."

And there it was, three years into their relationship, finally a clue into what made her husband tick. She yanked on her arms again, still manacled by his hands. "Let me go."

He let go of one of her arms but only to move his palm to her back, her other wrist still held firmly in his grip. His gaze latched on to hers. "Kiss me right now without emotion, and I will call the pilot to fly us out of here before the day is done."

She recognized it for the ploy it was. "I'm not playing that game, Coburn."

"It isn't a game. If you can prove to me there is no connection left between us to build on, I give you my word we will leave."

She stared at him. At the matter-of-fact expression on his face. Surely she could do that. Surely after what he'd done to her that night at his apartment, she could kiss him without emotion. All she needed to do was channel the intense hatred she felt for him in that moment and she'd be out of here, *free*, because she knew if she stayed the consequences would be worse.

Her gaze met his. "Let me go."

He uncurled his fingers from around her wrist but kept his palm to her back. His earthy, spicy scent from his morning run filled her head, reminding her of far too many hot, sweaty encounters with the man who held her. She took it as a warning, channeling a Zen place she didn't even remotely feel as she curved her fingers into his powerful biceps for balance.

She stood on her toes, pressed her lips to his firm, beautiful mouth in a light pressure that was in no way threatening, then pulled back.

"There."

Amusement glittered in his eyes. "Try a real kiss, Diana."

She swallowed the urge to claw his eyes out instead. He was such a bastard. He wouldn't kiss her that night in his bed, but now she was supposed to kiss him without emotion?

She took a deep breath and focused on the sensuous curve of his mouth that had always fascinated her. A man with a mouth made for kissing had been her initial impression of him, and it hadn't steered her wrong. Coburn loved to kiss. He used to make out with her for the better part of an evening when they'd worked together on the sofa, before finally carrying her to bed. That was why when he'd refused to kiss her that night, it had felt like a total and complete rejection of everything she was…

Blanking her mind to the low, tight pain that tugged at her insides, she caught his lower lip between her teeth and tugged. It might have been a bit more punishment than pleasure, but he played along, opening up for her. She slid her mouth against his, this time in a caress meant to stimulate. His hand pressed firmer against her back as he gathered her into him, returning the kiss with a steady pressure that signaled his complete acquiescence. She stiffened at the contact, because wasn't she supposed to be the one in control here? But then again a kiss involved two people, so she had to be okay with that.

Except then the weight of his solid, thickly muscled thigh moved between hers, the power of his corded muscles far too stimulating…

A few more seconds, she told herself, not about to be the one to cut this off so he could accuse her of reneging on their deal. She cupped his jaw in her fingers and dragged her mouth across the sexy contours of his, taking back control of the kiss. He felt like heaven, that was the problem. The soft, seductive, expert caress he gave back was one only Coburn knew how to give, as if he had all the time in the world to seduce her. It was everything she'd wanted when he'd taken her that night in his apartment, every bit of reassurance she'd craved that he was as much under her spell as she was under his.

It shattered her. Sucked her into a maelstrom of emotion she didn't want to feel—memories of how very good they had been together when it had just been them worshipping how they made each other feel. How nothing could touch her when she was in Coburn's arms because he was a part of her.

His palm at her back urged her closer into the V of his hard thighs. Deeper and harder the kiss went. When he urged her lips apart with the pressure of his and his tongue sought hers, she moved toward him, sliding her tongue along his in an unhurried, erotic movement she knew he liked. A shudder went through his big body. "That's it, baby," he murmured. "More."

A shiver rocked through her. The way she could make him feel made her feel a little too invincible. Soothed the raw edges he'd left the night he'd set out to prove he didn't care. Because it made him a liar as much as her.

She fitted her hips to his and rocked against his blatant arousal. The feel of him rubbing against her through the thin barrier of her silk robe sent a bolt of electricity to her toes. The taste of him, that essence that was distinctly Coburn, captivated her, enticed her on, his low growl into her mouth as he palmed her buttocks and held her still pulling a whimper from her throat.

The sound brought her crashing back to reality. She tore her mouth from his and flattened a palm against his chest. "No."

He let her go. As if he'd made his point. Her gaze landed on his lust-infused blue one. On the rise and fall of his chest as he struggled to get his reactions under control. She bit back the confusion raging through her, threatening to bubble out of her, but it was too late. The satisfaction glittering in his eyes told her he already knew.

"You see," he rasped, wiping the back of his hand across his mouth, "*that* is what I am talking about. When you crawl inside of me and it's so real it's like you *are* inside of me, Diana. *Tell me* you will share that with someone else… Tell me you think it can get better."

She couldn't. She could not deny it when she felt so *lost*.

"Take me home," she said quietly. "We can work this out, but take me home."

"No." He crossed his arms over his chest, his expression hard and implacable. "This is where we learn to sacrifice for the greater good. We leave our selfishness at the door and give our child the future he or she deserves. And the first step of making that happen is learning to understand each other because we clearly never did."

She stared at him, knowing on some level he was right, but afraid to admit it. Afraid what this might mean for her sanity to try again with Coburn…

His mouth flattened at her continued silence. "I've had clothes put in your closet, including a bathing suit. I suggest you put one on while you think about doing the *right* thing. I have some cooling off to do."

Her gaze dropped to his rampant masculinity straining against the confines of his shorts. It should have made her feel better to know he'd been as caught up in that as she had. Instead, she felt confused and on the verge of tears. She swallowed the feeling of helplessness that invaded her as she watched him walk away, so familiar and yet such a stranger to her now.

Her mind was too full to think, the late-morning sun

already so hot the silk robe was sticking to her body like a glove. She wanted to thumb her nose at Coburn, to protest by going to her room and staying there, but the thought of being inside instead of on the breezy beach was intolerable. It seemed there was no way out of here.

She put on one of the bikinis hanging in the closet in her room, grabbed a protein shake from the well-stocked refrigerator in the kitchen and went down to the beach. A perfect stretch of golden sand stretched in front of the cottage, bounded by two high cliffs that rose in a dramatic collage of crashing waves, sparkling sun and rough-hewn rock. It was a view that must have cost its owner millions.

She wondered what Arthur Kent would think if he knew Coburn was holding her prisoner here. Would he care? Or would he bow down to the Grant influence as everyone else on this godforsaken earth did?

Frustration seared her bones. She stalked past Coburn, who was just a blip in the turquoise water, his powerful arms cutting a path through the sea far out in the breakers. Who did he think he was? He could not do this to her. And yet he was.

She kept walking until she reached the end of the cove. Stowing her empty protein shake on a rock, she went for a dip in the sea. The warm water slipped over her limbs like a silken gift from heaven. Something like sanity returned as she flipped over on her back and floated on the waves. She stayed there for a long time, her negative emotions draining away with the lull of the surf and the sun.

A villa sat perched on top of the cliff, sparkling in the sunlight, looking so ethereal surrounded by the clouds it brought to mind a house of the gods straddling the earth and heavens. Did it belong to Arthur Kent? It certainly would be the view she'd choose.

Perhaps Coburn would introduce her to their hosts when

they returned on the weekend. If she hadn't found a way to do smoke signals and get herself rescued before then…

Her mouth curved. At last finding something amusing about her intolerable situation, she pulled herself out of the water and went to sit on a big rock to dry off. Leaning back on her palms, she contemplated the endless horizon of blue. Allowed herself to consider what Coburn was proposing. She couldn't deny reconciling with him and bringing up their baby together would provide the optimal environment for their child. Studies had shown that children were better off in families with parents who stayed together as long as the situation between the couple was on a reasonably agreeable footing. What changed that prognosis was when the relationship became toxic; when the environment was more harmful to the child's well-being than beneficial. Then a couple was better off separating.

She thought about what Beth had said about her and Coburn. That sometimes the most passionate relationships were the ones that burned out the brightest because of the intensity of the emotion involved. It was so true for them. They had never had a middle ground. It had always been highs and lows: one minute they were completely wrapped up in each other, the next they were at each other's throats.

Because they had refused to compromise. Coburn had been right about that. They had *both* been too selfish, too wrapped up in their own desires to want to give.

She closed her eyes against the brilliant power of the sun. As altruistic as she'd like to believe her work, as much as she hadn't had any choice in the crazy hours her residency had demanded, she had a choice now. Surgeons had families. They made it work. Yes, having a baby put a dent in your career. No matter what the Pollyanna types liked to say, motherhood slowed your ascent up the ladder. She'd heard male doctors make comments in the surgeon's lounge about dilettante mothers who didn't take their careers seriously. There *was* a stigma about it in the still-chauvinistic surgical community.

But none of this changed the fact that she was pregnant *now*. She either brought this child up with Coburn in a loveless marriage based on sex or they negotiated joint custody and passed the child back and forth like a tennis match.

She grimaced. Neither sounded appealing. To live with Coburn knowing he would never love her the way he once had would tear her heart out. Treating her child like a pawn in their separate agendas seemed equally distressing. *Unless* she found a way to control her feelings. Unless, she expanded in an "aha" moment, she took her emotions out of the equation. Which would by definition mean no sex. Just a convenient partnership to bring up their child.

Not what Coburn had been envisioning, surely, by his speech on the plane. But the only way she could play this without ending up a victim of her feelings was to negate them.

She thought about what she'd said to him. About marrying again… Thought about how completely he had owned her just now when she had kissed him. There would never be a man like that for her again. He was right. You came across that once in a lifetime if you were lucky. She'd had her turn.

What clinched it for her finally was Coburn's statement about giving their child a better emotional base than he'd had. *She* wanted that. She wanted her baby to grow up with parents who cared about his or her emotional well-being—parents who didn't treat their offspring like a chess piece in the game of marriage. Parents who cared about more than what grades the child brought home or what school he or she got into.

Her eyes fluttered closed. In that, she and Coburn were united. Not a bad thing to devote your marriage to.

When the sun got too hot to take, she stood up and brushed the sand from her limbs. For the first time in a week since her doctor had uttered those momentous three words, she had clarity as she walked back along the beach. Her husband might not like her plan, but that was all that was on offer. He could take it or leave it.

CHAPTER EIGHT

AS THE SUN dipped into the sea in a spectacular orange and crimson ending to a brutally hot day and the scents of the island descended over the cottage in a dozen different perfumes that stroked the senses, Coburn was just about to tell the cook his wife was feeling unwell and ask if she would take a tray up to her room when Diana appeared on the deck overlooking the water.

She had changed into one of the filmy, understated dresses Arthur Kent's PA had left in her room for her, the fuchsia silk dress embroidered with tiny white flowers making her look delicate and untouchable. His eyes narrowed on her ultraslim figure. The dress was too big for her even though it was her usual size. She had lost weight. She had not been well, and that needed to stop for the sake of their baby. She *would* listen to reason.

He watched as she walked to the railing that overlooked the rolling waves and rested her elbows on the edge. Her back was ramrod straight, the haughty tilt of her head at a fighting angle. Was it that much of a bitter pill to come back to him for the sake of this baby? Was being with him that distasteful?

His lips compressed into a tight line as he clenched his hands by his sides. Until she'd left him in a move he could never have anticipated, he had always thought his rocky road with Diana would level out. That these were the hard years with them where they were finding their way and they would learn to compromise. He had been in a state of shock when she'd left, if the truth were to be known. He had expected her to come back to him as she always did when they fought, when she gave in to the inevitability that was them. But days had grown into weeks, and when he had finally called to end the standoff, she'd refused to speak to him.

His mouth curled in a grimace. His naïveté was staggering. The belief that if you loved someone enough you could overcome the differences that had ultimately pushed you oceans apart.

Something low and heavy stirred in his gut. He had tried so hard to put this woman out of his head. And still she tied him in knots.

"Give us fifteen minutes," he murmured to Lucie, the cook.

Snaring the bottle of nonalcoholic champagne he'd chilled from the refrigerator, he took two glasses from the cupboard and joined Diana on the deck.

The fading light cast his wife in a golden glow as he came to stand beside her at the railing. "Is your nausea anything to worry about?"

She turned to face him, her dark lashes fanning down over her cheeks in a wary look that said the fight was not over. "It should settle down in a few weeks."

"You've lost weight. Isn't that hard on the baby?"

She shook her head. "Lots of women lose weight in the first trimester. I'll gain it back quickly when the pregnancy accelerates."

He caught the agitated gleam that flared in her eyes. "You're nervous."

"Of course I'm nervous. In nine months, maybe less, I'm going to be bringing a new life into the world. A child that is totally dependent on me for everything, every minute, every hour of the day."

"Us," he corrected, setting the bottle and glasses on the table beside him. "*We* are having this child. You aren't alone in this, Diana."

"I love how men say that," she mocked. "You aren't the ones carrying the baby. You aren't the ones suffering the debilitating nausea and you aren't the ones sleep deprived from getting up in the night."

"Because we can't," he pointed out. "But there *is* such a thing as a bottle and we can take turns."

Her gaze skimmed over his perfectly pressed shirt. "I can just see it now. You walking the living room floor at two in the morning with the baby draped over your shoulder as you rehearse your presentation for the next day."

He lifted a shoulder. "I will."

"Right. And when you start leaving zeros out of numbers and cost the company millions it'll still be all good."

He scowled. "Now you're being ridiculous. This goes to the issue of control and you hating the fact that you're losing it."

She waved her arms around them. "And what is *this*? What would your slick tongue call this? *Persuasion?*"

"Reason," he returned with a sigh. "I thought the afternoon might have put you in a better mood."

"What? Lounging in the sea and sun is supposed to make me forget you've kidnapped me to make me see your way?"

He elected not to answer that, instead picking up the champagne and uncorking it. She flicked a glance at the bottle. "I can't have any of that. Another joy of being the one carrying this baby. At least if I could drink, I could *tolerate* you."

"This is nonalcoholic."

"What are we celebrating? You forcing me into captivity?"

He lifted his gaze to hers. "We created a baby together that night at my apartment. I thought it was time we acknowledged the fact."

The husky edge to his voice caught him off guard. He kept his eyes on hers, his words hanging on the air between them like a challenge—a statement he dared her to refute. She stared at him for a long moment as if deciding which way to go. Finally, she inclined her head. "It is… something to celebrate."

He handed her a glass of the bubbly. "I'm glad we agree on that."

She touched her glass to his and took a sip. He took a mouthful of his own and pointed his glass at her. "Have you come to a decision?"

"Yes." A closed, impenetrable expression passed across her face. "I agree it would be better for us to bring this child up together. *If* we can remain civil with each other. I agree we need to learn to understand each other better in order to do that. But I have ground rules."

His gaze narrowed. "What kind of ground rules?"

"The only way I will agree to do this is if we do it on a strictly contractual basis. We will be together for the sole reason of raising this child. We will behave amicably toward each other, but there will be no *sex*."

A wave of incredulity swept through him. "You expect us to remain married but not have sex?"

"Exactly like that." Her mouth curved as she echoed his favorite expression.

It took him a moment to find a response to that, it was so…*ludicrous*. "I think," he replied slowly, "that you are forgetting it was you as much as me initiating our sexual encounters."

"Not anymore." She lifted her delicate, stubborn chin.

"I refuse to engage in emotional warfare with you, Coburn. I've had a lifetime of it already. If we're going to raise this child together without creating a war zone, we need neutral ground."

"So in other words you're being a coward."

"No, I'm being smart. A self-preservationist. We both know how you can rip me apart with the easiest of efforts. You did it that night at your apartment. That's what *started* all this. So now we take it out of the equation."

"Let's just be clear here," he countered, his tone edged with a warning note. "You *started* it that night. Not me."

"Funny how you learn from your mistakes."

He crossed his arms over his chest and leaned back against the railing. "So I'm supposed to be in a marriage with no physical gratification. How do you think that's going to work?"

"You were the one giving the lectures on self-sacrifice. Or was that just you talking and me listening?"

He thought about how she had taken him apart inside earlier with that kiss he hadn't allowed himself the night their baby was conceived. How, in using that as a weapon against her, he had allowed her to penetrate *his* defenses. He may be as on board as her about avoiding emotional entanglement, but sex wasn't something he could do without.

"All right," he said quietly, holding her defiant gaze. "We play it your way until you decide you want to change the rules. And when that happens, I will be acquiescent in your hands, sweetheart, because I will be *way overdue*."

Antagonism flecked her smoky gaze. "I will not change the rules, Coburn. I'm the one who stayed away for a year. I'm the one who filed the divorce papers, remember? I have willpower."

"Do you?" He closed the distance between them until they were mere centimeters apart. Her breath fanned across his cheek, quickened when he dragged his thumb over the pulse point at the base of her throat. "I don't see the point in denying ourselves the very potent physical connection we share."

"I do," she said grimly, holding herself perfectly still under his touch. "I've told you my conditions."

He brought his mouth to the shell of her ear. Felt the tremor that went through her. "Why? What is it you need to hide so badly from me? What hurt is buried so deep inside of you, you can't let me near it?"

She pressed a hand to his chest and stepped back, a glitter in her eyes that said he'd struck a nerve. "How about we reverse that? How about we go upstairs right now, strip down and while we *do it*, you tell me why you run from everything? Why you hate family get-togethers with your mother so much? Why you and Harrison are always at each other's throats? Why bicycling in the Alps is preferable to getting to know my family so you might not hate each other?"

His mouth curled. "You read too much into things, Diana. My mother is a cold fish of the highest order. Your parents hated me from the start, so why should I bother? And my brother and I are close again, thank you for asking." He lifted a brow. "Does that cover it all?"

"Not even close," she breathed. "So hating my parents means you won't be there to support me?"

"*Did you support me?* About half of the gossip columns in New York predicted the demise of our marriage before it happened because you were *never* by my side. I had a wife who was a *mirage*."

"You had a wife who was a resident. A *resident*, Coburn. The doctor who does everything and more because we aren't senior enough to do anything but take it." Her eyes glittered like black diamonds. "I was exhausted, I could hardly put a foot in front of one another, and you kept pushing, pushing me until I cracked. All you had to do was wait five years, *five years*, and things would have leveled out. But your ego, your desire for attention, couldn't do it."

He clenched his hand tight around his glass. "If you mean my ego couldn't handle being put second to your job *every single time*, then yes, that's true. You shut down when you work, Diana. You put every single bit of emotional energy you have into your patients, and when you get home, there's nothing left for me." He waved a hand at her. "Men are simple creatures. Throw us a bone every once in a while and we're good. But you didn't even have that for me."

The color drained from her face. She looked pale, so very pale standing there in front of him. It made his guts twist. But this was a necessary conversation, long, long overdue.

"You're right," she said finally, "I didn't. I expected you to understand the demands of my career. To let me put my future, *our future*, first until that tough period was over."

"While I spent five years in a relationship with *myself*?" He shook his head. "Life is too short for me to sit by while you learn the meaning of balance, Diana. Begging for affection is not my style."

"While I was begging for *support*. Begging for help getting through the five toughest years of my life."

"And then what? You would have convinced Frank Moritz to give you that fellowship and it would have been another two years of hell while you obsessed about being perfect for him. When was it all going to end? You have this need to prove yourself I don't understand."

"Because you run away from your need to do the same." She threw the words at him, bitter honesty ruling her now. "You hated that your father gave Grant Industries to Harrison to run. Instead of fighting for it, instead of proving to Harrison you should have equal footing, you pretended you didn't care. Well, I care. I will not apologize for caring. I will not apologize for wanting some security in my life so when *you* decide you don't want me anymore, I have something to fall back on."

His mouth dropped open. "What the hell are you talking about?" She slammed her mouth shut. He closed the distance between them, capturing her jaw in his fingers. "Why would you say that? Give me one reason that would have ever led you to think I would have left you. *One*."

Her gaze dropped from his. "It would have happened eventually. You were constantly disappointed in me. I could never give you what you wanted."

His fingers tightened around her jaw as rage swelled inside him. "This is not about my disappointment in you. This is about *your* history with your parents. I *worshipped* the ground you walked on, Diana. I would have done anything to make our marriage work. But how was I going to do that when you were so busy staking out your territory so you could run the minute things got bad?"

"It wasn't like that."

"It was *absolutely like that*." He let go of her jaw and stepped back before he truly lost it. "What else did I need to do to make you feel secure? What else, because it is *beyond* me?"

"You could have kept your hands off those women." She yelled the words at him, the champagne in her glass tipping over the side in her fury. "You could have kept it in your pants long enough to convince me that I meant something to you, Coburn. That I wasn't replaceable as easily as your next flavor of ice cream."

His vision clouded over as he clenched his free hand at his side. "You walked out on me, remember? I tried to call you. I tried to make things right and you wouldn't have me, so *do not* accuse me of being unfaithful."

"*Weeks* later. After you'd already been with those women."

Fury tunneled through him, flaying every centimeter of his skin. "See, that's where you're wrong. Because I can't help but remember the timing. It was after you threw my attempts to talk in my face for about the fifth time that I got the message and satisfied my needs elsewhere. You made it clear you didn't want me, so I took what I needed."

She blinked hard. Stared at him for a long moment before she looked away. "I hope she was good, Coburn. I hope she satisfied your slavish devotion to your needs so you didn't go without."

"I would have *preferred* my marriage was intact, but I didn't have that choice."

Color leeched from her cheeks. She turned away from him, rested her forearms on the railing and drew in a deep breath. "Rehashing all of this isn't going to help us move forward."

"I beg to differ. I'm finding it highly illuminating. Who knows? If we put all our cards on the table, we might even find some clarity."

"With a card counter like you?" She kept her gaze on the horizon, where the sun had sunk so low it was about to be swallowed up by the sea. Her skin looked too pale in the dying light, her shoulders set high in a defensive posture, her mouth a brittle line. As if a surge of wind might blow her away.

"We should eat," he said roughly. "We can continue this conversation over dinner."

"I'm not very hungry. Maybe I'll just go straight to bed."

"You will eat." His harsh tone brought her head around. "There is no running from things you don't like this week. We are facing them head-on."

Something flickered in her eyes, but she didn't argue. Likely because she knew she had to keep her strength up for the baby rather than any form of obedience. He pulled out a chair for her at the candlelit table Lucie had set on the deck, then settled into the one beside her. Her gaze flicked to the chair opposite her as if she'd rather he sat there, and it made him smile inside. Letting her get comfortable wasn't part of his plan. Infiltrating her was.

"We need to buy a proper home," he announced, filling their water glasses.

"I heard a business associate is selling his town house down the street from me. It actually has a yard. Maybe we should take a look at it."

Her hand paused midway to her water glass. "I'm not living in Chelsea."

"A fifteen-million-dollar townhome isn't good enough for you?"

"Not if I'm bumping into your castoffs in the park."

His mouth quirked. She'd be shocked at how few of those women he'd taken to bed. Everyone would.

"My discards won't be strolling in the park at midday."

"I'm not living in Chelsea, Coburn."

"And I'm not living on the East Side. Maybe we split it down the middle and go somewhere neutral? The Upper West Side perhaps?"

Lucie set their salads down in front of them. The scowl disappeared from Diana's face long enough for her to give the cook a smile. It disappeared when she left. "I need to think about it. It needs to be somewhere central for me for work."

"You don't have a job. And you won't for a few years to come."

"You've decided that, have you?" She picked up her fork and pointed it at him. "I have a career, Coburn. I've spent fourteen years studying to become a surgeon. Maybe *you* should stay home and I should work."

"And that would make sense since you just quit your job, you're the one having the baby who'll need the recovery time and I just took the job as CEO of a multibillion-dollar company."

"You're the one preaching sacrifice."

"Not on this. Yes you will go back to work, but the early years for a child are crucial. You know that better than anyone. You can go back to work when they're in grade school."

"*Grade school?* That would kill my career. Who's going to want to hire me after five years away from the knife?"

"What's the alternative? Do you want our child to be raised by a nanny?"

A flush filled her cheeks. "I don't know. I need more time to think about it."

"*I* do. I was raised by a succession of nannies. My father worked every waking hour of the day and my mother spent all her time laying the charitable groundwork to be a politician's wife. I will not have our child raised like that. We will be emotionally *and* physically present for him or her."

Her hand fisted on the table. "Me working doesn't preclude that."

"Yes it does. Your job is all consuming and you know it."

"I can work part-time."

"And how does that work out for most of the surgeons you know? Then comes the phone call at two in the morning and you're out the door. You need to be realistic here."

"Coburn—"

"It's not happening. You have to start acknowledging your limits, Diana. *Now.*"

She blinked hard and stared down at her plate. He watched her in astonishment. Were those tears? Tears of anger or real tears?

She looked up at him. The stormy expression in her ebony eyes gave him his answer. "I found out a week ago that my life as I know it is going to change irrevocably. I gave up my dream in Africa because of it and have agreed to give this marriage a shot for the sake of this baby. But if you continue to push me like this, I will walk the minute we set foot in New York and you *will* be talking to me through our lawyers."

He took in the defiant angle of her chin. The fierce glitter in her eyes. She meant it. "All right," he said, holding up a hand. "I'll back off, I promise. But we need to make these decisions soon. Finding a house in New York is going to take time."

"Wrapping my head around all this is going to take time. Give me some space."

He proved he could by making small talk throughout the rest of the meal and ensuring she put food in her mouth, albeit a small amount. By the time they got to dessert, she looked as if she was going to fall asleep in her seat. When her eyelids closed for the third time in a minute, he pushed back his chair and stood up. "Bedtime."

Her eyes flew open.

"For you," he drawled. "Although you know I am available whenever you have the urge."

She scowled at him and stood. Swayed slightly. He stepped to her side with a lightning-quick reflex and slid an arm around her waist. "What's wrong?"

She took a deep breath, her eyes fluttering closed in a far-too-pale face. "I just stood up too fast."

He frowned as she leaned into him. "Does this happen a lot?"

"It's my cardiovascular system catching up." She took a few more breaths, then stepped away from him. She didn't look much steadier on her feet. He cursed and slid an arm under her legs and back to pick her up. Her protests ringing in his ears, he carried her inside and up the stairs past a wide-eyed Lucie, who probably thought they were destined for a night of hot sex. He wished.

"This is unnecessary," Diana muttered as he shouldered his way into her room and nudged on the light. He set her down on the carpet, keeping his arm around her because she still looked far too pale for his liking. She extracted herself and looked expectantly toward the door. "Thank you."

He shook his head. "I want you in bed first. Otherwise I'll have visions of you keeling over in the bathroom."

"Coburn, I'm fine."

He sat down on the bed and crossed his arms over his chest. "Go brush your teeth."

She marched off to the bathroom and shut the door with a loud thump. He turned the bed down and waited. When she came back a few minutes later, her cheeks had recovered a bit of color. "You can go now."

"Get undressed first and into bed."

She shook her head. "Out."

"I don't take orders from fainting pregnant women."

"I didn't faint."

He set his jaw.

She muttered an expletive under her breath, raised her arms and stripped off her dress. His gaze drifted down over her lacy white bra to her flat stomach. "When will you start to show?"

"Not for a while."

She reached past him for her nightshirt. He caught her hand with his, bringing it to the curve of her stomach. Her breath hissed from her throat as his fingers flattened across her warm, silky skin. His baby was in there. His baby. A surge of emotion passed through him, almost blinding in its intensity. Up until this point, he had felt only anger and frustration, but *this*, this was something else entirely. Elemental. *Powerful.*

He raised his gaze to Diana's. Something passed between them then—the knowledge that they had created this together. That no matter how mixed up they had been when they had made this life, it was about to transcend them both.

He moved his gaze back up over her breasts, straining against the lace of her bra. They were swollen, larger than the handful he'd always coveted, the tips of each peak stained a darkish red-brown.

"Your body is already changing."

Her nipples hardened beneath his gaze. Her cheeks were filled with a rosy color when he lifted his eyes to hers. She curled her fingers around his hand on her stomach and pulled it away, confusion darkening her eyes to inky black pools. "Leave, Coburn."

"Why?" A husky note infiltrated his voice. "You know how much easier this would be if you let me get under your skin."

"Easier how? So you can have your way?"

He immersed himself in the hazy, conflicted desire shining in her eyes. "Because of all the things we've screwed up, *this* has always been right."

"No." Her denial pierced the air between them, an iron edge to her vehement tone. "This is what we do, Coburn. We use sex to cover up all the other things that are wrong with us. If you truly want this to work, it has to be about more than that."

"See, that's where you and I see it differently." He reached up and tucked a wayward chunk of her hair behind her ear. "For me, sex is part of the solution."

She turned and reached for her nightshirt. Stripping off her bra with maximum efficiency, she pulled on the short, less than feminine cotton shirt he'd always hated, hiding her curves from view. But not before he got a perfect silhouette of her ripe, swollen breasts, which woke his frustration from that afternoon up in a hurry.

"How about," he offered silkily, dropping his gaze to

her bare, delectable thighs, "I just take care of you? The way you like it best? It would put you to sleep…get all that frustration out. We don't even have to call it sex."

Her face turned the color of a ripe tomato. "Get out of my room."

He shrugged and strolled to the door. "Call me if you change your mind. I'm just around the corner."

The bad word she uttered under her breath made him smile. "Oh, and, Diana…?" He turned around, absorbing her mutinous stance, hands clenched by her sides. "I'm expecting us both to bring things to the table this week. Things that will help us bridge this divide between us. So use the time between now and tomorrow to think of what you want to address. Questions you have for me, things you hate about me… This is your chance. But be ready by nine. I'm taking you for a sail."

"A sail?"

"Arthur has a beautiful sixty-five footer. Assuming you still remember how to man a boat?"

"I'm rusty, but yes. What does this Arthur do if he owns million-dollar islands and beautiful yachts?"

"Airlines. Railroads. He's an old friend from my cycling days."

She eyed him. "So this is what we're going to do? Address our marriage like a grocery list?"

He lifted a shoulder. "You took sex off the table. I'm just following your lead."

He left then. She needed rest. And if he wasn't going to spend his night buried in his wife's delectable body, he had a handful of pressing emails to address.

He took a glass of brandy into the library, sat down at the desk and flicked on his computer. But he couldn't seem to focus. His head was too busy processing the raw and unabridged version of his marriage according to his wife. She had chosen to call out "irreconcilable differences" on the divorce papers sitting in his office, which would have made sense to him given their different philosophies on life. But unbeknownst to him, she had also apparently spent their entire marriage waiting for him to call it quits and walk out the door. *Just as her father had.*

Heat moved through him. He was nothing like Diana's father. Wilbur Taylor was a megalomaniac with a god complex that came from being a world-renowned surgeon everyone treated like a rock star. He considered everything and anything in this world his domain, including the women in it, his affair with a fellow surgeon simply being the longest standing of his string of indiscretions. Yet Diana's mother had chosen to stay. Why?

He took a slug of the brandy, twisting the chair to look out at the sea, now shrouded in darkness, its great mass an inky pool you could lose yourself in a million times over. Wilbur Taylor's infidelities were just one reason he didn't respect the man. The way he treated his daughter had been inexcusable to him, the tactics and subtle threats he had used to nourish Diana's need for perfection coming at the cost of her happiness. So that she would follow in his footsteps—so that she wouldn't let the family name down.

It had always taken him hours to soothe Diana after a visit with her parents. *That* was why he disliked them so much. That and the fact that Wilbur had never considered him good enough for his daughter…

His mouth curved in a bitter twist. How would Diana's father react now if his daughter had brought him home with stars in her eyes? Perhaps the newly minted CEO of a Fortune 500 company, instead of the overlooked second-in-command, would meet with his approval? Would have been a suitable alternative to the young surgeons Wilbur had kept shoving down Diana's throat even after they were married.

He sat back in his chair and took his brandy with him.

It would make sense given her family history that his wife might have harbored a fear he might do to her what her father had done to her mother if, *at any time*, he had given her pause to doubt him. *If* he had spent his time admiring other women as he'd watched Wilbur Taylor doing. Instead, he had consistently deflected the attention of women who hadn't cared if he'd worn a ring on his finger or not because he was rich and good-looking and being a wealthy man's mistress wasn't the worst gig in town.

He hadn't needed to stray. He'd loved his wife. He hadn't given any of those women more than a passing smile when Diana had abandoned him on social nights out for work. And yet here she was *doubting* him? His supremely confident wife who had never been fazed by the women who had chased him.

What were those women to you? A salve for your embittered soul? A way to prove I meant so little to you?

Her words from the night they'd conceived their baby came back to him. He had taken it as her usual arrogance. *Bitterness.* What if it had actually been a whole other side of his wife he'd never known existed? A vulnerability at her core she'd never displayed. The fact that she'd left him, *shattered* him, when he'd taken those women didn't seem to matter. In her eyes, he had proved her right all along.

A fatalistic feeling enveloped him as he ran his finger along the blunt edge of the tumbler. How would he know? The woman he had married had been a total enigma he'd thought he could one day solve and never had. The woman he'd removed from Africa another Diana again. Who was the real Diana? He'd be damned if he knew.

The ocean stared back at him, dark, silent. *I could do an emotional autopsy on you and I'd still never get to the bottom of you.* Had Diana been right? Had he been just as guilty of not showing his true self to her? Had he even known who he was? Taking over Grant had changed him.

Had illustrated just how lost he'd been since his father's death. However cutting Diana's appraisal of him had been, she had been right about him not fighting Harrison for control of Grant. About him running. He hadn't wanted any part of a power struggle with his brother. Wasn't sure a legacy that had seen his father blow his brains out was something he wanted.

If there was something he had over his wise older brother, it was the knowledge that life required living. To tie his identity to a role, to a job that was inherently vulnerable to any number of agenda seekers, was not how he wanted to live his life. He wanted that elusive balance no one ever seemed to find.

He finished the brandy on a last smooth, fiery gulp. He knew his future now. He intended on making Grant the most powerful car-parts manufacturer in the world, so indelibly the analysts would stop comparing him with his saintlike brother and recognize his brilliance for what it was.

But that wasn't what he was *here* to do. He was here to put his marriage back together, and that involved some truth on his part, as well. He had used those women to get Diana out of his head. To satisfy the numbness he craved. And, admittedly, if he was to be honest, to punish her for leaving him.

He had been addicted to distraction. Addicted to never letting himself care because that had been the example set for him by his own parents.

Had it cost him his marriage?

A chime sounded an incoming email. He pushed his focus back to the screen of his computer. And read the email that changed everything.

CHAPTER NINE

"BRING HER AROUND!"

Coburn's shout was eaten up by the roar of the wind and the water. Diana nodded and eased up on the headsail to turn them toward the cove he was pointing to. The thrill of commanding such a big, beautiful boat washed over her like a shot of adrenaline. She tacked sharply again to bring them all the way around so they were headed directly into the mouth of the bay. Her blood pumped in her veins as they sped over the sea like the smoothest of silk. She'd forgotten how much she loved the spray of the water on her face, the freedom of flying across it and how perfectly she and her husband worked together when it was just them, sweating it out in tandem to master the elements.

Riding a strong gust of wind, the sleek sixty-five footer cruised toward the shore. Coburn eased off on the mainsheet and slowed them into an easy, graceful glide. Expertly, effortlessly he brought them within striking distance of the shore, and they dropped anchor.

She helped him secure the boat, then dropped to the sun-soaked deck, her breath coming in shallow, harsh pulls. Her limbs felt weighted down, heavy. She leaned back on her forearms and took in deep, restorative pulls of air while Coburn went downstairs to get their lunch. This pregnancy was not only making her nauseous, it was zapping her of all of her energy.

It was nearly one o'clock, the sun blazing right above them in a perfect, cloudless blue sky. She drank in the idyllic little cove they were moored in. Surrounded by palm trees and bounded by a stretch of pristine white sand beach, it looked as if it had never seen a human trespasser.

They were in the British Virgin Islands, Coburn had revealed this morning, nestled within a cluster of private islands owned by the world's richest men. Inaccessible to anyone but those issued an exclusive invitation to explore such nirvana.

She closed her eyes and drank in the heat. Her husband emerged from below deck with a picnic basket and two glasses, a pair of low-slung navy swim trunks and a Yale T-shirt his only adornment. His innate grace, the way the athlete in him used his strong, muscular thighs to steady himself as he moved across the swaying boat, drew her eye. The sun was already picking up his natural tendency toward a swarthy, dark complexion, emphasizing the magnetic blue of his eyes, no less hypnotizing than the vast sea behind him.

He was still the most physically beautiful male she'd ever encountered. Hands down.

"All yours, sweetheart." He caught her stare, dumping the picnic basket beside her and lowering himself to the deck. "Take what you will."

She closed her eyes to the magnificence of him. She'd lain awake after he'd left her last night thinking about his offer. Thinking about how she *shouldn't be thinking about it.* He was utterly unselfish when it came to pleasing a woman, wickedly sensual in his methods.

"You can't help it, can you?" She jumped as he purred the words in her ear. "Was my offer last night a little too tempting?"

"Hardly." She shimmied to the side to put some distance between them. "I meant what I said, Coburn."

"You forget I know every variation of you. Every expression. *That* was lust."

She closed her eyes. "It's the pregnancy hormones talking."

The sound of the waves lapping against the boat filled her ears. His soft laughter joined it. "I had no idea pregnancy increased a woman's sex drive. I would have thought the opposite."

Her cheeks fired with a warmth that had nothing to do with the sun. *This* was the last conversation she wanted to be having with him when sex was most certainly off the agenda. When she was still angry at him for assuming she was going to give up her career while he played the golden-hued CEO.

She focused her gaze on him. "I have a question for you."

"You did your homework. Good girl."

She rolled her eyes. "I want to know why you agreed to take the CEO job at Grant when you said you never wanted it."

He cracked open a Perrier bottle and handed it to her. "I decided I wanted it."

"Why? What changed your mind?"

He shrugged. "It was clear the business community was going to back Harrison's run for president. The only question was whether he would take it. I needed to be ready with my answer, and I realized that answer was yes, I did want Grant to be mine. It's in my blood. But I wanted to do it my way, not Harrison's way, not my father's way."

"And now? Do you think it was the right decision?"

He frowned. "I'm only six months in. I am not my brother. There are growing pains… But yes, I think it was the right thing to do. I'm excited about the future."

She could sense it. There had always been a restlessness about her husband, a low-level frustration with anything that had to do with work, because playing second fiddle to his brother had never been easy for him. The intense, focused man beside her now was a very different creature. She had seen it in him instantly that night at Tony and Annabelle's—the ruthless edge that made her all jittery inside.

"Harrison is not an easy act to follow."

He shrugged. "It's like comparing apples and oranges. Harrison was a known quantity—steady, dependable. He rarely worked outside of the box. With me, the board isn't sure what they're getting. I'm doing things differently. I've ruffled some feathers. It's going to take time."

She studied him then, the tension etched into the grooves at the sides of his mouth. His father, Clifford Grant, had been an icon of American business, a success story that was corporate folklore. Harrison was so widely respected he had been chosen to represent the interests of business in a presidential race. It made the pressure her father had put on her seem like child's play.

"What was that phone call this morning? You looked stressed."

He cracked the other bottle of Perrier open and took a long gulp. "Just business."

She scowled. "Is it just me playing this game or have you checked in, too?"

He swiped the back of his hand over his mouth. "This is about me and you figuring this out, Di, not business. I'm not interested in sidetracking the discussion."

She thought him sharing why he had been distracted all morning *was* them understanding each other, but she left it for the moment. "Fine. I would like to understand you and Harrison. You would never explain what happened between you two."

Dark lashes swept down over his brilliant eyes. "We've had some major philosophical differences over the years. Although, like I said last night, we've worked a lot of it out."

"Philosophical differences over what?"

"Does it matter?"

She gave him a pointed look. "You don't get to veto every topic I throw out there."

He set the bottle down and crossed one of his long legs over the other. "My father's illness put a strain on all of us for many years. Harrison and I were focused on keeping things running when my father was in a depressive state and out of the picture and attempting to keep the ship upright when his brilliance was running amok. We were a good team. But after my father shot himself, everything changed between Harrison and me."

The fact that Coburn's father had been a severe manic-depressive for many years before he had committed suicide was something she'd known. But she'd thought the rift between him and Harrison had preceded that, had been because his father and Harrison had such similar personalities and, according to his mother, had been closer than he and Coburn.

Her husband sat back on his forearms and looked out at the sea. "Harrison pretty much lost his mind. There were... extenuating circumstances around my father's death. It was a period during which he was hell-bent on expansion, intent on stealing market share from competitors. He made a deal to buy a company from a Russian named Anton Markovic. Outwardly, it was an excellent deal. What my father didn't know was that Markovic had sold him a false-bottomed company. It wasn't until after the deal had closed that it became clear the company was pretty much worth nothing.

"It wouldn't have been a big deal," he continued, "if Grant hadn't been so highly leveraged. It nearly bankrupted us."

"Couldn't you have gone after Markovic?"

"We tried. He declared bankruptcy shortly thereafter."

She sunk her teeth into her bottom lip. "Your father blamed himself."

He pulled his gaze from the water and brought it to rest on her face. "It was a perfect storm. He lapsed into depression, the stress of the run for governor hit him and he took his life."

A lump formed in her throat. "Oh, Coburn. I'm so sorry."

"Harrison was the one who found him, sprawled over his desk. I've never seen a rage even come close to him that night. He tore my father's study apart. He went for the gun in the safe. An eye for an eye, he said."

Her breath caught in her throat. "He was going to kill Markovic."

"I managed to talk sense into him. But Harrison vowed he would destroy Markovic the same way he had destroyed our father. I told him to let it go, that he would destroy himself in the process. That nothing would ever bring our father back, but it was this holy grail for him, the only thing he ever wanted. It blinded him to anything else."

"He spent seven years laying the groundwork, until we had rebuilt Grant and Markovic had risen from the ashes. Then he quietly bought up every global supplier Markovic had to cripple him, to destroy him. He arranged a meeting with Markovic in Washington last year, intent on bringing him to his knees face-to-face. But he didn't do it."

"Why?"

A wry smile curved his lips. "I'd like to say he finally listened to me, but I think it was Frankie. He said she was his conscience."

She absorbed the horrific, tragic tale and what it must have been like for Clifford Grant's two boys to go through it. To watch their father shattered like that and the shame they must have felt along with their grief. She had always known her husband was a product of his heartbreaking past, that his need to be in constant motion was motivated by a consuming desire to forget. But only now did she understand how much that night must have colored his life. *Shattered* him.

"And what of you, Coburn?" She pinned her gaze on his face. "If you didn't have vengeance to fuel you, how did you cope?"

He shrugged. "I moved on. Righting a wrong with another wrong is never a solution. Harrison hated that I felt that way, hated that I wouldn't back him in his plan. He thought it showed a lack of loyalty. But selling my soul to the devil was something I wouldn't do."

He had run instead. Her heart broke a little bit more for him.

"Why didn't you ever tell me this?" she asked quietly.

His gaze skipped away from hers. "You don't need to know our dirty family secrets."

Something throbbed inside her at that. "I'm not an expert at this, obviously, but isn't that what we're supposed to do? Confide our deepest, darkest secrets with each other so we can deal with them together?"

"Like you do?" he shot back. "You apparently spent our entire marriage thinking I was going to walk out the minute things got hard and yet you never thought to inform me of how you were feeling."

"I have now," she returned evenly. "It's clear how little we actually communicated about what really mattered. We were too busy fighting about everything else."

He was quiet, his gaze raking over her face in an intense, indigo-blue perusal. "Why hasn't your mother left Wilbur? Why does she let him humiliate her like that?"

She blinked at the sudden turn in conversation. It was an answer she had to think about. "She said she loved him," she finally responded. "That her marriage hadn't turned out the way she'd expected it to, but that was life."

"That was life?" An incredulous look spread across his

face. "Your mother is a beautiful, charismatic woman. She could find someone else in a heartbeat."

Her mouth flattened into a grim line. "My father kept telling her it was the last time and she kept believing him. When I called her on it, when I was old enough to understand just how twisted it all was, she asked me what she was supposed to do. She gave up her career for him. She gave up *everything* for him because his life was so demanding, because she had me to take care of. And then you're fifty and it doesn't seem so likely you're going to walk out and find someone else."

He shook his head. "It still doesn't make sense to me. Where was her pride?"

"In appearances. My mother idolizes my father. She belongs to the cult of Wilbur Taylor. She thinks he's just being a man. That every marriage has its issues."

"And you think I'm just like *him*." He raised himself up on one elbow and scored her with his gaze. "You asked me that night on the terrace if those women were a salve for my embittered soul. You want the truth, Diana? The real truth? *Yes.* Yes they were. I used those women to try to forget you…to get over you. They were *your* collateral damage. Because I was hurting. My wife had walked out on me. My marriage was *over*."

She stared at him, her head spinning at the unexpected admission. She had always suspected the woman had been just that for him, but marking them *her* collateral damage?

"Do not use me as an excuse for your behavior," she said sharply. "You are fully responsible for that."

"You're right," he agreed. "I did it all on my own. I have to take responsibility for it. But you don't get to act hurt and self-righteous about it, not when you relinquished your claim on me in such an abrupt and decisive fashion. The blame goes both ways, sweetheart."

She clamped her mouth shut. She had no idea she'd hurt

him so badly. She'd thought he was looking for an excuse to get out of their dysfunctional marriage with that argument they'd had. But his raw emotion now came from the very heart of him—emotion she'd never seen him exhibit. And for the first time since she'd walked out on him, she allowed herself to consider the fact that she had been very wrong in leaving him. That he was as good at hiding his emotions as she was.

He pushed himself upright, his hand reaching for hers to tug her to him. Her chest collided with the heat of him, her fingers coming up to grasp his biceps. His gaze when it latched on to hers ran roughshod through every defense she had. "You have to get over it," he said roughly. "Those women meant nothing to me. I apologize, Diana. I apologize for unwittingly digging up your past and hurting you. I apologize for my behavior the night we conceived our baby. But now is the time to wipe the slate clean. Now is the time to build on what we do have to make this work for the sake of our baby. But you have to let me in."

Her stomach contracted. She knew he was right. But the thought of him making love to, *having sex* with those women… She wasn't sure she could ever get over it.

"I want to hate you for it…those women." The words tumbled out of her mouth before she could stop them. "I see it in my head and I want to be physically ill."

His face grayed. "Then, we are both grappling with what we think is the unforgivable. For the sake of our child, we need to move past it."

She swallowed hard. He still had feelings for her, however much he tried to hide them. He was saying everything she'd wanted to hear that night she'd gone to that party before ending their marriage. Except that he still loved her.

He was willing to slug it out together for their baby. To attempt to meet somewhere in the middle of their radically different approaches to life to make this marriage work.

Was it enough?

Would not having all of him ever be enough?

She rolled to her feet. “You promised me time. Give it to me. No more subtle seduction, no more pushing, no more manipulation of everything I say. Just give me the time I need and I promise you I will consider this.”

His eyes darkened. He jerked his head in silent accord. She walked to the edge of the boat, slipped off her shorts and dived into the cool, heavenly turquoise water.

Her head knew what she had to do. Now she just had to get her heart to agree.

CHAPTER TEN

COBURN WAS TRUE to his word. For three days and three nights he did not touch her, goad her or push her to discuss anything more pertinent than the weather and what they were going to do that day. They interacted like polite acquaintances who happened to have an intimate knowledge of every inch of each other they kept tightly in check as they explored the island by boat and foot.

When they'd had enough of the ever-present baking heat, they headed for the crystal clear water and the coral reefs that surrounded the island. Diana could have spent days there swimming with the schools of brightly colored fish, avoiding her problems. And yet, funnily enough, by letting her mind go and relaxing, clarity came instead.

Her life had been irrevocably changed when she and Coburn had conceived this baby. She had to give them a second chance. A chance to forgive each other their transgressions, as Coburn had said, and perhaps find some level of happiness.

A clammy feeling attacked her appendages as she sat lounging by the pool with a book on yet another stunning Caribbean day while her husband worked in the office. She was terrified. A powerful voice inside her couldn't help pointing out the parallels with her mother and father's relationship. It would only ever be Coburn for her. Did her weakness for a womanizer like her husband make her as much a victim of the cult of Coburn as her mother was for her father?

The realist in her knew she was risking her heart. The optimist was sure her husband felt more for her than he was willing to admit and they could build on that.

Coburn finally made an appearance as the late-afternoon shadows chased each other across the surface of the pool. He wore the same distracted, aloof look he'd sported for days now, this new foreign version of her husband that eluded her attempts to reach him. Always with Coburn there had been emotion, whether positive or negative throughout their roller-coaster highs and lows. He was an extrovert, a man who needed to express himself as much as she needed to crawl inside herself at times.

She swam toward the edge of the pool and clutched the side, studying the tension etched in his face.

"I thought you were going to be in there all day."

"I'm sorry. There's a lot going on." His gaze singed her skin as it moved over her curves in the coral bikini. "You're burning."

She looked down at her shoulders. They were a bit pink. Coburn offered her a hand and pulled her out of the pool. She bit her lip as he wrapped a towel around her. "You could share, you know."

"I won't distract you from the choices you need to make."

She lifted her chin to look up at him. "I'm willing to give this a shot, Coburn. I'm willing for *us* to give this a shot. But this is it. We make it work this time or we walk away. I grew up in a war zone between my father and mother, and I won't put a child through that."

The tense line of his mouth slackened. "And you are going to let me in? Trust me?"

She nodded. "I am committed to making this work. But I won't give up my job. A huge issue in our relationship was not being able to give for the other person's needs. I want to be there for my child, but I'm not prepared to put my career on hold until they're in school. My skills would never recover from it."

A war went on in that dark blue gaze of his. "Nonnegotiable," she underscored.

"You don't trust me. You don't trust us."

"It's not about trust. It's about my identity, what I love doing. I need to practice."

He tucked the towel tight around her and let go. "All right. We compromise." His gaze held hers. "We've screwed up a lot of things, Diana, but I promise you we will not screw this up. It's too important."

Their marriage had been important, too. She forced herself to nod before the panic rising up in her throat enveloped her. "I know."

He inclined his head. "Arthur is back. He's invited us to dinner tonight with some friends. Are you up for it?"

Her mouth curved. "So you'll let me loose now that I've fallen into line?"

He moved his gaze over her. "I'd prefer to indulge myself on a whole other level and forget the socializing entirely. But since Arthur is a good friend, it will have to wait."

Her insides were still vibrating from her husband's clear indication of exactly where their relationship was going in short order as Diana dressed for dinner with the Kents. She didn't know why she was so nervous to embark on a physical relationship with Coburn again. She'd done it that night at his apartment when they'd conceived their child. But this time it was about walking into it with her heart open. Fully invested. She felt as if she was twenty miles out in that sea sparkling outside her window and being told to swim for her life.

She pressed clammy palms to the soft, clingy fabric of her dress. Its sea-blue color reminded her of her husband's eyes—rich and endlessly fascinating.

Coburn was waiting for her on the terrace when she arrived, ridiculously handsome in a white shirt and dark trousers. His eyes as they ate her up suggested her nerves were highly warranted. Measuring, calculating, they swept over every curve of her body in the sexy dress, lingering on the swell of her newfound cleavage with an uncensored appreciation that made her knees wobbly.

Her steps slowed as she approached him, hesitation written in every line of her body.

His gaze moved back up to her face. Cataloged what he found there. "You look…devastating."

She swallowed past the dryness in her throat. "Thank you."

The polite response her mother had taught her to issue upon receiving a compliment rather than stammering out a quick denial as many of her teenage friends had came out stiff and unnatural. Coburn's brow rose. He took the last couple of steps toward her, his fingers curving around her jaw as his other hand settled on her waist and pulled her close.

"I'm getting the feeling my ever-poised wife is nervous."

"Hardly," she denied, her reply coming out a bit too breathless for her liking.

His fingers slid to the hollow of her nape. "I thought we were going for honesty here. If *I* was being honest I'd say that blowing off dinner to make love to my very beautiful wife is highly tempting."

Her insides dissolved into a pool of molten heat. "Coburn—"

He dropped his mouth to her ear. "The only question

would be how and where I would do that. I'd be willing to explore more than one option."

She put a hand to his chest and leaned away from him, her head and heart full of way too much everything. "But we *are* going to dinner. It would be rude not to."

His gaze studied her face. "Yes we are. But first I'm going to kiss my wife."

Her heart sped up in her chest. The hand she had pressed against his torso couldn't decide whether it wanted to keep him at a distance or allow him closer. He took the decision out of her hands, splaying both palms across her jaw to hold her in place while he brought his mouth down to nudge hers apart. She froze, her lips immobile against his. It was like walking into a tsunami with your eyes wide-open. She wasn't sure she could do it.

His fingers tightened around her jaw. "Open your mouth," he demanded. "Let me in."

The war went on in her head, the battle between her two selves loud and chaotic. And then she couldn't fight it anymore. Her lips softened beneath his. He took them in a deep, drugging kiss that swept away all conscious thought except for the intoxicating, deliciously male scent of him, the tall, strong length of his body that brushed hers tantalizingly close, but not nearly close enough. His taste, his touch was achingly familiar and yet different somehow. As if the exceedingly tough, driven man he'd become had seeped into every part of him, and even his kiss couldn't help but be affected by it.

She drank him in, relearned every contour of his sensual, beautiful mouth.

He murmured her name, his voice a velvety caress that slid across her sun-warmed skin. His hands shifted lower to her hips to drag her against him. She moved into him, luxuriating in the press of his strong, muscular thighs against her. Only with Coburn could a kiss be this soulful.

His hands moved over her buttocks, shaping her against him. Froze. "You have nothing on underneath this dress?"

Heat flared in her already warm skin. "It's impossible with it."

He brought her chin up with the tips of his fingers, the heated shimmer in his eyes making her insides quiver. "It wasn't a complaint," he drawled softly. "Knowledge is power. Or pleasure, in your case..."

She bit down hard on her lip. How could she forget what he did with such knowledge? A dinner party on a steamy night in Manhattan filled her head. Coburn had just been back from a business trip to Germany. He'd touched down, driven home and changed, just in time to walk out the door with her to a cocktail party. Intensely sexual in nature, her husband had spent the evening trying to keep his hands off her, but a week away from each other had taken its toll. She had excused herself to use the powder room when Coburn had discreetly followed her, slipped in after her and locked the door. He had taken her against the wall, swift and hard, his raspy voice in her ear telling her how much he'd missed her. How he had pleasured himself thinking about her in his big, lonely hotel room.

"Hot, wasn't it?" Her husband's husky taunt returned her focus to his face. He was studying the heat staining her body a bright red. "It was the most uninhibited I've ever seen you."

She pulled in a breath. "Behave."

"For now," he agreed, a pirate-like smile curving his lips. "This time I want you very verbal, sweetheart, so I know I'm satisfying your frustration to a suitable level."

Her stomach contracted. Skipping the party suddenly sounded like a good idea to her, too, because his blunt seduction was going to have her in tatters after an entire evening of it.

"But first," her husband drawled, nixing that idea as

he stepped back and reached into his pocket, "you need to put this on."

She stared at the shiny object sitting in his palm. The symbol of so much happiness and angst housed in a plain, shiny gold band gleamed back at her like a point of no return. Her wedding ring. Actually, her second wedding ring if you were to be technical about it. The first she'd lost scrubbing for surgery, something Coburn had never forgiven her for.

"You kept it."

He picked up her left hand and slid the ring on her finger. She had never seen the practicality of a large diamond with the job that she had, so it had only ever been this simple band that had declared her his.

Their gazes met and held as she looked up. "This time it stays, Diana. Through the good and the bad."

She wondered which would prevail for them. Coburn bent his head to her ear. "Stop thinking and enjoy the evening."

She gave it her best shot as he guided her to the car and drove up the hillside to the fabulous Kent villa perched on the cliff. Her speculation from that day in the sea was confirmed. The view from the low-lying, Italian-inspired structure was outrageously stunning. Sheer rock face plunged down to pristine, glittering stretches of golden-sand beach, where white-foamed waves crashed up onto the shore in a testament to the power of nature.

Coburn had told her Arthur had purchased the island for ten million dollars five years ago. A ten-million-dollar view it certainly was.

A butler directed them to the terrace that overlooked the sea. Torches burned brightly, illuminating a crowd of perhaps a dozen guests with champagne glasses in their hands. The wealthy elite of Arthur's world, Diana pegged them, the perfectly coiffed hairstyles of the women and the exquisite cocktail dresses they wore as casually as if they'd stuck a hand in the closet and thrown on the first thing they came up with, telling. As were the jewels that sparkled from their well-tanned skin.

A tall, thin man with an elegant stature broke away from the group and came toward them, a smile on his face. His features were expressive rather than handsome, a crooked nose highlighting his sharply drawn, aristocratic features. Arthur Kent, she surmised, from the warm greeting he gave her husband.

Inquisitive hazel eyes turned to her. She had the sensation of being thoroughly analyzed before Arthur bent and pressed a kiss to both her cheeks. "So I finally get to meet the lovely Diana."

"You have a very beautiful home," she said smoothly. "Thank you for allowing us to visit."

He lifted a hand. "You are welcome anytime. I keep telling Coburn that, but he is too caught up in the rush of being a big-time CEO now to take me up on it."

"Not too busy to pick your brain tonight," Coburn responded, a wry smile curving his lips. "I would like to if you don't mind."

She wondered if her husband wanted to ask Arthur for his advice on whatever was happening at Grant that was making him so distracted. She wasn't to find out as Arthur's wife, Dana, joined them along with their two young boys. Nine and seven, Maciah and James were utterly charming miniature versions of their dark-haired British mother, who was easily twenty years younger than the airline magnate. A trophy wife, she wondered, because surely she was stunning, but Diana quickly saw it was much more than that. The Kents were a vivacious, happy clan who had moved to the island upon Arthur's early retirement to escape the pressures of their former life. It was clear they had learned the secret of living, and it was not based on how much money they had in the bank.

When Arthur told the sports-obsessed boys Coburn had played competitive soccer in school, they pleaded with her husband to kick a ball around the yard. Never one to resist a sporting activity of any ilk, Coburn passed his drink to her and good-naturedly trailed after the two rambunctious boys.

"You don't have a drink," Dana commented. "Shall I get you a glass of champagne?"

"Actually, orange juice and soda would be lovely."

A speculative glimmer entered her hostess's eyes but she was too polite to comment. She went off to retrieve the drink from the bartender while Diana and Arthur watched the boys chase Coburn around the yard. Her husband expertly faked and deked, keeping the ball out of their possession with tricks that made them laugh and chase harder. The tension faded from his face for the first time in days as he laughed along with them.

"He's good with children." Arthur rested his forearms on the railing and watched the game. "He told me once he wasn't sure he wanted any. I thought that strange given his love of life. He jumps into everything with his head and heart fully immersed, damn the consequences. It's a great example for a child. Fear kills so many dreams."

How true. It had stifled hers until she'd identified what she truly wanted out of life, and that was to work with kids. To do something exceptional with her skills in Africa, where too many were denied basic health care. And perhaps, she thought, it had killed her marriage the first time around because Coburn was right. His ability to see through her made her feel naked and vulnerable. His ability to make her *feel* terrifying. It was why she'd run away. She knew that now.

Her husband let out a roar of laughter as the two boys

pulled on his pant leg to try to bring him to the ground, fierce determination on their young faces. He *would* be a good father. With Coburn, life was an adventure waiting to happen. His joie de vivre when she'd met him had been so opposite to her own careful, controlled nature that she had been blown away by it. Amazed someone could live in the present like that when she'd known as a teenager what her next two decades would look like.

But somewhere along the way their separate agendas had collided and her husband's lust for life had gone from being charming to infuriating. Now with more pressure on him than ever before and saddled with a baby he hadn't even wanted, how would he react? Would it be too much for them?

She swallowed past the knot in her throat. She couldn't think like that. She had to be positive about this if it was ever going to work.

"They tire you out?"

Arthur joined Coburn on the lawn as he held his hands up, declaring himself done with the impromptu soccer game.

"They're fast little devils," Coburn conceded, taking the cold beer Arthur handed him. "I haven't been to the gym nearly enough since I took over Grant."

Arthur tipped his glass at him. "It's all consuming, isn't it? Why do you think I got out when I did? The secret is balance, my friend, and it's not easy to find."

Coburn took a long sip of his beer and stared out at the jaw-dropping view of the vast blue horizon. "Ever handle a recall?"

His mentor nodded. "More than I would have liked. You up against one?"

He nodded. It was highly confidential, early days yet,

but he knew with Arthur it would go no further. "It could be a big one. Any advice?"

"Get out in front of it. Get the facts, make your assessment, and if you have blame to take, carry it with big shoulders. These can make or break a company's reputation."

He knew it. He wasn't sleeping because of it.

He picked Arthur's brain on his experiences until the internet billionaire from the neighboring island stole Arthur away for a discussion on boats. His wife was standing with their hostess and two other women on the far side of the patio. He joined them just in time to catch the tail end of a discussion of Caribbean real estate as the wives of the internet baron and a software CEO debated their favorite islands.

"Do you have a preference, Diana?" the diminutive, very beautiful internet baron's wife asked.

Diana smiled. "I love the Turks and Caicos. My parents have a place there. Unfortunately it would be difficult to live in the Caribbean with my profession."

"Oh. You *work*?"

His wife stiffened under the hand he held to her back. "I do. I'm a surgeon in New York."

"A surgeon?" The CEO's wife wrinkled her brow. "You mean a 'cut people open with a knife' kind of surgeon?"

"Exactly that," his wife confirmed. "With a purpose in mind, of course."

The other woman didn't seem to get his wife's dry sense of humor. "That's very…impressive. I bet Coburn is wowed by you."

"That's one way of describing it."

He slid his hand down to her waist and pulled her into his side with a reprimanding squeeze of his fingers. "I most certainly am. Beauty and brains are a definite turn-on for me."

"I'll bet they are." The blond girlfriend of another neighboring millionaire who looked young enough to be her fiancé's daughter gave him an appreciative once-over. She had been throwing him sideways looks since he'd arrived, making him wonder if her man needed to pop a few pills to satisfy her. "My husband tells me you run one of the world's largest automotive companies, but I wouldn't understand what it is really because it's all that stuff *inside* a car."

He smiled. "Very well put."

"Do you work?" his wife piped up. She hadn't gotten any less stiff beneath his hand. The urge to drag her off somewhere to loosen her up was an idea.

"Oh, no," the blonde pooh-poohed. "We have two children. I don't get these women who work when they should be home. Parenting is the most important job in the world. You can't bring back those years."

His wife went ramrod straight. "No, you can't," she agreed. "But if there were no female surgeons we'd have a serious shortage of doctors to take care of *your* children. And then where would we be?"

The blonde shrugged a shoulder. "It worked just fine when women were at home."

The other woman must have read the antagonism painted on his wife's face because she swiftly backtracked. "Oh, I wasn't talking about *you*," she demurred. "I'm sure you're fabulously talented. I just think women take it a bit far sometimes…forget their priorities."

Diana's fingernails bit into his side. Sensing an imminent explosion, he gave the other two women a smile. "Would you mind if I steal my wife away for a moment? I wanted to show her something before dinner."

Without waiting for a response, he nudged his wife forward. "Don't let her get to you," he murmured. "What is she going to say? She doesn't have your skills."

"You'd rather I be like her," she muttered. "I should be

at home lying on the bed eating bonbons waiting for you to come home."

"Don't give me ideas." He slid his hand lower to cover her bottom. "If I thought I could have you spread out and waiting for me when I walked in the door I would, but I think the world is better off with your surgical skills."

She looked up at him, a fierce glitter in her beautiful brown eyes. "Don't flatter me to get me to cool down. I am not a button to be pressed."

"Oh, yes, you are," he countered silkily, his palm shaping her bottom. "And I intend to press every last one before I'm done with you tonight."

Her eyes widened before her long lashes fanned down over her cheeks to cover them. "Why don't you go press the young blonde's buttons? She'll be more than willing I'm sure."

Temper rose in him, swift and sure. He stopped at the railing that overlooked the sea and stepped close enough to cage her in. "This is the last time I'm going to say this, Diana, so *hear me* when I tell you I have no interest in any other women. Nor will I in the future, even when you are round with my child. *You* are the only woman who can turn me inside out. *You* are the only woman I want warming my bed. That's always been the way."

Her breathing fractured as he stood with arms on each side of her on the railing, his heated gaze holding her in place. The darkening of her eyes to almost black said he might finally have gotten his message through.

"Say it once more," he promised, electing to hammer his message home while he had her attention, "and I will find a room, a *corridor* to convince you of it."

His wife's body went slack against the railing. The glitter in her eyes said she wanted him as badly as he wanted her. That corridor wasn't a half-bad idea.

"Dinner is served." Arthur walked past them on his way

to alert the other guests, an amused expression on his face. "Unless you have another type of sustenance in mind."

Diana's face went beet red. He stepped back and guided her to the table set under the stars. His wife was primed and ready for him. Good thing, too, because his own very primed and ready body had had enough.

Diana was seated to the right of her husband at one end of the long, rectangular table laid with ornate silver place settings and tall candelabras. Dana sat at the head of the table to her right, thankfully keeping her across the table from the blond temptress. If she'd had to sit beside that lipstick-encrusted wolf in sheep's clothing she might have burst a blood vessel.

As it was, she was having difficulty relaxing with her smoldering, very sexy husband by her side. He seemed determined to take every opportunity he could to touch her as he passed the butter and filled her water glass. His threats had made her stomach churn with a sexual awareness of him that was getting worse with every minute that passed.

She focused desperately on her hostess, who it turned out was a very talented artist who painted scenes from the islands sold for high price tags in a London gallery. The surgeon in her loved hearing about the creative process and how she worked with her hands to achieve certain effects.

At some point after their salad plates were cleared and before the main course was laid down, Coburn's hand landed on her thigh. She stiffened as his warm fingers curved into her heated flesh, staking a firm ownership. She might have kept her composure had he not moved his hand down to her knee during the main course and gradually worked her dress up her thigh. She flashed him a look full of daggers, but he went innocently on talking to Dana as if he wasn't seducing her at a table of twelve diners.

And really? Did she want him to stop? She swallowed

hard as he slid his palm between her thighs and worked them apart. Her muscles gave way of their own volition, trembling in low-grade anticipation as his calloused fingers scraped against her skin. It seemed difficult to pull air into her lungs, to maintain even the simplest of conversations with heat descending over her in waves.

She put her silverware down on her plate, laying it neatly across the china as if to signify the discipline to stop. "Coburn," she murmured in his ear. "No."

"Sound more convincing," he rasped back, "and I will."

She couldn't do it. His thumb dipped into the heat at the core of her, his swift intake of breath telling her he'd discovered just how aroused she was.

Oh. My. God. She attempted to coherently answer Dana's question about a jewelry boutique in New York her hostess couldn't remember the name of while Coburn's thumb found the honeyed, delicate nub at her center and rocked against it. Her breath seized in her throat, her hand fisting on the table.

Somehow the name of the store popped into her head. She told Dana, who pulled out her smartphone to make a note of it. Coburn's caress deepened, quickened. She clenched her thighs around his hand, her mind warring with her body. She could not let him do this here. She could not.

She slipped her hand under the table, closed her fingers around his and squeezed. His fiery blue gaze met hers, and for a moment she was lost. He was as gone as she was.

His hand slipped away from her skin. Her constricted chest eased, oxygen making its way back into her lungs. Coburn tucked a lock of her hair behind her ear and leaned in close. "You are so ready for me, baby," he murmured. "Do not expect me to hold back."

Her nervous system short-circuited. She ignored the unabashedly curious looks the blonde threw in her direction and focused on breathing. She took absolutely nothing in as their dinner plates were removed and dessert and coffee were served. The anticipation simmering in her veins was of the all-consuming variety.

Arthur had just asked the table if anyone would like a refill on the nightcap when a bundle of small boy appeared on the terrace in his pajamas and threw himself at his father. Maciah, Arthur's nine-year-old son, babbled some incoherent words to Arthur, bringing the entire table to a halt.

She thought it was a night terror at first. The little boy's eyes were wide and he was hyperventilating, trying to pull air in. His father pulled him onto his lap, smoothed his hair and told him to take deep breaths.

Maciah's small chest inhaled and exhaled. "James is hurt," he sobbed.

His father frowned. "He's in bed."

The little boy took another deep breath, his voice shaky as it tumbled out. "We wanted to have some fun, too, so we decided to build a fort on the cliff. Only James fell and hurt himself."

The internet CEO's wife gasped. Diana sat up in her chair. Arthur took his son's face in his hands. "James is on the cliff?"

"Y-yes. Daddy, there's all sorts of blood."

Diana was on her feet. "Call an air ambulance," she instructed Dana. She flicked her gaze to Maciah. "Can you show Daddy and I where James is?"

He nodded and slipped off his father's lap. They raced outside and over to the edge of the cliff in front of the house, which was bounded by a tall fence. Maciah slipped through an opening she hadn't seen. Diana followed, Arthur and Coburn behind her. Her heart lurched as Maciah pointed to a jagged ledge about five feet down from the edge, the sheer face of rock beneath it terrifyingly steep.

James was lying on the ledge, barely visible in the darkness, his ragged sobs piercing the night air.

"We need light," she said tersely. Someone ran up to the villa and came back with a flashlight. She shone it down on the ledge, her pulse accelerating at the awkward angle the boy's leg lay at, but more so because of the amount of blood spurting from it. He had ruptured an artery.

"Is the ledge steady?" she asked Maciah.

He nodded. Coburn cursed. "You don't know if it will take your weight."

"We're about to find out."

He caught her hand in his. "I'm going down first. If it's stable you can come down."

"Coburn—"

"Nonnegotiable."

She held her breath as her husband levered himself over the edge of the cliff and down onto the ledge with the stealth of a man who had climbed some of the world's biggest peaks. Arthur looked as if he was in shock, his face white as Coburn stood up gingerly, testing the steadiness of the rock.

"It'll take both of us."

She sat on the edge of the cliff, turned and eased herself down, Coburn spotting her with a hand to her back. She knelt beside the gray-faced little boy, forcing herself to ignore how high they were over the rocky shore. Using her fingertips, she found the source of the bleed and pressed down hard to stem the flow. It was the femoral artery. A major one. *Not good.*

"Take off your shirt," she ordered Coburn. "I need to bind the wound."

When he didn't respond immediately, she flicked her gaze up to him. He was staring at all the blood. *"Coburn,"* she bit out under her breath, "I need binding material *now*."

Her husband emerged from his trance, tearing his shirt

down the front. He shrugged it off and started ripping it in strips. She grabbed the first one and bound it around the little boy's thigh to stop the bleed. An agonized cry escaped James. "More," she ordered Coburn. "Give me as many as you've got."

She glanced at the little boy's chalk-white face, worried he was going to go into shock. "James," she said softly, "did you know I'm a doctor? That I put people back together again?"

His lips trembled but he didn't acknowledge her. "So you've hurt your leg," she told him gently. "It isn't anything we can't fix. We just need to get you to a hospital so we can do that. You'll get to ride in a helicopter. Won't that be fun?"

His weak nod was a good sign. She reached for the strips Coburn handed her. "I'm going to tie your two legs together to stop them from hurting so much. Can you be brave for me?"

He nodded on a little sob. She set her jaw, knowing it was going to be painful for him, and went to work. It was her job to be immune to the little boy's tears, but his terrified wails as she stabilized his broken leg against the other tore at her heart. They were hundreds of yards above a rocky shore. His leg had been spouting a waterfall of blood. She got it.

She secured James's legs. Coburn climbed up on the cliff so Arthur could come down and talk to James with her until they heard the whir of the helicopter blades. She climbed up on the cliff then, so the ambulance crew could get the little boy on a stretcher and pass him up onto solid ground.

It wasn't until everyone was securely on firm ground and James was being loaded into the ambulance that her knees buckled. Coburn caught her, sliding an arm around her waist.

"I'm terrified of heights."

"I know."

The raw emotion in his gaze brought tears dangerously close to the surface.

"You are insanely brave, Diana Grant."

She didn't feel brave. She felt very close to the edge, too much emotion attacking her from every direction.

The ambulance crew secured James. Arthur stepped into the back to go with them. Coburn bundled her into the car and drove down the mountain. Diana looked out the window and thought about what could have happened. That little boy could have taken a wrong step and…

"It didn't happen." Coburn flicked her a sideways glance. "You can't live your life in *what-ifs*."

"Is that what you think I do?" she asked quietly.

"Until you decided to drop yourself into war-torn Africa, yes. That was a departure."

It had been. She sat in the car when they pulled into the driveway of the cottage, in a complete state of inertia. Coburn opened the door and reached down to scoop her out of the seat. She didn't argue, merely rested her head on his chest as he let them into the cottage, carried her upstairs and deposited her on the floor of his suite's bathroom while he turned on the steam shower. She looked down at her dress. It was so stained with blood it might as well have been red, not blue.

She reached around to unzip her dress, but her hands were shaking too hard to accomplish the task. Coburn moved behind her and brushed her hands out of the way. The whisper-soft touch of his lips against the sensitive skin between her neck and shoulder sent a shiver down her spine. "You were a goddamned superhero tonight."

She shook her head. "It's my job."

The rasp of her zipper raked across her heightened senses. "It's not your job to walk out on ledges when you're terrified of heights to save a little boy. You didn't even blink."

Another shudder vibrated through her. "I was so terrified something would happen and we would plunge into the water."

"But it didn't stop you." He pushed her dress off her shoulders, his hands coming up to cup her breasts while his mouth returned to that spot that drove her crazy. "I have never been so proud of anything or anyone than I was of you tonight."

Her heart squeezed. "I have skills, Coburn. I need to be using them."

"I know that." He pressed his fingers into her shoulders and turned her around. "I have continually underplayed your job. I've never fully understood until tonight when I saw you with James how amazing what you do is."

Something that felt a lot like hope sprang to life inside her. Maybe this could work between them. Maybe they could change. Maybe she just needed to stop thinking, stop analyzing as she always did and follow her heart. Give them a chance.

Coburn unhooked her bra and tossed it to the floor. His heated gaze roamed over her swollen flesh, the greedy edge to it making her insides quiver.

"I swear to God that scene at the dinner table nearly set me off," he muttered, sliding his thumbs over the partially puckered peaks of her breasts to bring them to aching erectness. "You should have let me finish it."

Fire raced through her veins. "That was not happening."

"Now it is," he murmured in her ear. "Get in the shower, Diana."

She stepped into the shower, her jellylike legs barely holding her in the wake of his softly issued promise. The hot, heavenly spray poured down over her as Coburn stripped off his bloody clothes. She turned into the jets, letting the hot steam take her, washing away the nightmare of the past two hours.

Coburn stepped in behind her, the huge steam shower more than large enough for both of them. In fact she thought it might have been designed with half a dozen people in mind. But her husband wasn't keeping his distance. He washed himself quickly, then picked up the lemon-scented soap and started working on her. His hands built a lather down her back, over the curve of her buttocks, which he lavished with an inordinate amount of attention, and then the length of her legs.

He stayed kneeling at her feet as he nudged her to turn around. Then he ran the bar of soap over her calf, up her thigh and repeated the pattern on her other leg. When he cupped her between the legs, ostensibly to spread the lather there, his big palm squeezing her sensitized flesh, she moaned and leaned back against the wall. He stood and tossed the soap on the ledge, his muscular, powerful body pressing her harder into the tiles. His fingers wound themselves in her wet hair, his mouth claiming hers as he brought his hand between her thighs again, this time to claim her with the slick invasion of his fingers. She moved her hips against his hand, reveling in the pleasure he gave her with every smooth slide of his powerful fingers. The pressure built, and soon she was begging, *pleading* for release in incoherent little sentences. His mouth stilled on hers, his breathing rough against the hiss of the spray.

"I need to taste you, baby." His sexy rasp stoked the fire inside her, his eyes spearing hers as he drew back to look at her, a barely restrained hunger in his gaze. "Your sweetness…how I make you feel. It was all I could think about tonight touching you."

Her legs threatened to buckle. Coburn reached past her, shut the shower off and found a towel to wrap her in. She gave her wet hair a quick rub before he lifted her up, walked through to the bedroom and deposited her on the huge king-size bed. She felt like the prey of some large jungle animal as he joined her, intent written in his midnight blue eyes. Her stomach curled in on itself as he curved his palms under her thighs, bent her knees back and exposed her to the heat of his gaze.

She closed her eyes. It was too intense, all of it, to bear. She wasn't sure what was more erotic, how much she loved it when he did this to her or how much he enjoyed doing it.

The first slide of his tongue against her most sensitive flesh shattered any remnants of numbness, her body a desperate instrument for him to play. She arched against him, seeking, *wanting* more. He gave it to her with hot strokes of his tongue that laved her, devoured her, until every nerve ending in her body was centered between her legs, focused on what he was doing to her.

He wrapped her legs over his shoulders and delved deeper. She screamed; she couldn't help herself. His fingers bit tighter into her hips to hold her where he wanted her. "That's it, sweetheart. Give yourself to me. You taste so insanely good."

She buried her fingers in his wet hair to anchor herself as he shifted his focus to the delicate little nub at the heart of her. He slid fingers back inside her at the same time his tongue lashed over her clitoris with deadly intent. She arched into him, focusing on the release he could give her. When he pressed his fingers into her stomach and took her over the edge, her hoarse cry reverberated in her ears. The white-hot pleasure that radiated from her center to every nerve ending licked her up like an all-consuming flame.

"Oh, God," she murmured as the aftershocks of her orgasm racked her core, her hands fisting the comforter.

Coburn crawled up her body, his arms caging her on each side, a wicked grin on his face. "At your service..."

Her cheeks fired. "As if."

He brought his mouth down on hers, his erotic kiss exploring every inch of her mouth, blending the taste of her, of him, of the passion they shared. Her heart stuttered in her chest. The intimacy of it was blinding.

He lifted his mouth from hers and rolled onto his side. "Touch me," he told her harshly, his gaze locking with hers. "Feel how badly you make me want you."

She turned and focused on the fully erect length of him, brushing against the hard muscles of his abdomen. He made her mouth dry with anticipation as she curled her fingers around him, his silk-over-steel texture reminding her how good he felt inside her. And this time she got to enjoy him without a condom for the first time ever, no barrier at all between her and his magnificent virility.

The barely leashed impatience written across the hard bones of his face dissolved on a low growl as he pulled her hand away. He pushed her onto her back, then dragged her against him so his powerful body spooned hers. Her heart stuttered in her chest. He loved this position. Loved to talk to her as he made her crazy.

She relaxed her limbs, allowing him to push her top leg forward to give him the access he needed. The crown of his thick shaft pressed against her slick flesh, promising extreme pleasure.

"Tell me," he rasped in her ear. "Tell me you want me..."

She did because all week she'd been fighting this. Fighting the forces inside her that knew only Coburn could make her feel whole.

His fingers tightened on her buttocks as he sank into her, one glorious inch at a time, allowing her body to adjust to his size, his girth. She wished she could see him, see his eyes as he took her, but he was in complete control, capturing the delicate flesh of her earlobe between sharp incisors as he stroked his way inside her until he was buried to the hilt.

"I love the way you take me," he murmured huskily as she gasped with the fullness of his invasion. "So tight, baby. So perfectly made for me. Nothing was ever so perfect."

His words soothed her battered psyche. She reached back to touch his face. "I want to see you."

He ignored the request, withdrawing from her and entering again with a deep, hard stroke. His breath at her ear came quicker now, a roughness to it that said he was fast losing his grip on that ironclad control. She felt him everywhere in this position, touching every nerve ending, firing every synapse she had until her body clenched around his, begging in silent invitation.

"Coburn...I need to see you."

He pulled out of her and rolled onto his back, tugging her astride him. His eyes were the darkest blue she'd ever seen them as he looked up at her, inviting her to consume him as he had consumed her.

She took him in her hand and guided him inside her, sinking down on the rigid column of flesh. Her breath whooshed from her lungs as she absorbed all of him. He was sinewy, beautiful muscle beneath her, hers for the taking. But it wasn't enough. She wanted his soul. She wanted to know he was *hers.*

She ran a thumb across his beautiful mouth. "You wouldn't kiss me that night."

"It was your punishment."

She lowered her mouth to his. "Do it now."

He curved his palm around the back of her head and took her mouth in a scorching kiss that penetrated every layer she had until she was his and he was hers and nothing existed except the two of them and what they created together. Magic. Endless, sublime magic.

She lifted her mouth from his to circle her hips around his pulsing flesh, indulging herself with every hard inch of him. His flesh throbbed and swelled inside her, even larger if that was possible. She leaned forward and let the friction of her body rubbing against his take her close to orgasm. And then there was only Coburn and the pleasure he gave her. How treasured he made her feel when they were together like this.

Her eyes latched on to his luminous blue ones. "I've missed you," she admitted raggedly. "I've missed *this*."

He reached up to brush his thumb across her cheek, his fingers sliding down to cup her jaw. "Climb into me, baby. I've got you."

It was hypnotic, the glitter in his eyes as he unleashed himself and drove up inside her, his hands on her buttocks holding her steady. She couldn't take her eyes off his as she drank in the harsh edge to his breath, the ripple of muscle in his biceps as he held her above him. She let herself fall completely then, because in her heart she knew he had her.

When she was so close to a second orgasm but frustratingly not able to attain it, he moved his thumb between her legs to find her clitoris, his slick rubs across the tiny peak making her whimper.

She moaned her approval, squeezing her eyes shut as he methodically took her apart. The clench of her body around his ripped an oath from his throat as he throbbed inside her, then joined her, spilling his mark of ownership deep within her.

It was so different, so vastly intimate to have a piece of him inside her like this; it sent a sated, liquid warmth through her entire body. She snuggled into him when he turned off the light and curved her against his side. But her glow faded when he dropped off to sleep almost immediately. No low murmurs of love as he'd once whispered in her ear to put her to sleep, just the furnace-like warmth of his body to comfort her.

It was a vivid reminder they were together only because

of this baby. That this was what living with only half of him would be like. She'd had a taste of it now, and it was even worse than she'd thought it would be.

CHAPTER ELEVEN

ONCE, A COUPLE of years ago, Coburn had run a race in the Sahara desert, where the only goal was to emerge alive. It was the equivalent of completing five and a half marathons in five days in one-hundred-degree heat. You slept in a tent only long enough to give your body the rest it needed, then you got the hell out before some creature ate you alive.

He'd mused, upon finishing the race, that he'd likely never feel that particular sense of impending doom again in his life. He hadn't until now. It figured sleeping with his wife would do it.

Waking up with her long limbs curled around him, the sparkling Caribbean sunshine slanting over them through shutters he'd forgotten to close, it felt as if he'd come face-to-face with one of the deadly reptiles he'd been so careful to avoid in the desert.

Instead of amazing sex to cure his frustration, last night had been an emotionally complex coming together that had burrowed her under *his* skin that much deeper. She was getting to him exactly how she used to, and that couldn't happen. Not when she'd taken his world apart piece by piece once before. Not when he'd never allow her to do it again.

His chest getting tighter with every moment, he slid out from under his sexy wife, threw on running clothes and headed for the door. A hard, pounding run in the sand helped until he stopped, an hour later, and his head was still in the same place. Confused. Muddy as hell.

Maybe part of the problem was that his wife had been a goddamned comic book hero last night, throwing herself onto a ledge above the ocean and saving a little boy's life. It had hit him square in the face how much he'd underplayed the importance of her career. *He* couldn't have saved that boy. He'd been standing there frozen like a useless idiot until she'd prompted him into action.

She had blown him away. But then again he'd always known his wife was exceptional. He'd loved Diana's brain as much as he loved the rest of her. No one challenged him like her. No one.

He swiped his T-shirt across his dripping face and pulled in deep breaths as he walked it out to cool off. He needed to draw some lines. Needed to ensure he was in control of this marriage and not the other way around. Too much was riding on his performance as Grant CEO over the next six months to let himself fall back under Diana's spell. He had exactly what he wanted—her agreement to make this a proper marriage for the sake of their child. Now he had to make it work for both of them. Which meant no false illusions on either of their parts. The all-consuming love they'd once shared had destroyed them. This iteration would involve common sense. Reality.

His mobile buzzed in his pocket. He fished it out, glanced at the display and held it to his ear. "David."

"Sorry to intrude," his chief operating officer apologized. "I have Reg on the line, too."

His heart sank. Having his legal counsel on the line meant the recall had shifted from early rumblings into reality.

"How bad is it?"

"Bad," Reg responded. "The amount of vehicles affected is in the tens of thousands. The class action suit involving those injured is in the hundreds. We are currently trying to qualify how many of those claims are substantial and what percentage are being motivated by the large sums of money being thrown around by the lawyers. Suffice it to say, this will be the largest recall we've ever been involved in."

He closed his eyes against the nightmare unfolding on the phone. "How likely is it our parts were directly involved in the brake failures?"

"Very likely."

His insides twisted into a hard knot. Five deaths had been associated with the faulty breaking systems; five deaths Grant's hands were now stained with. He felt sick to his bones that his company was responsible for a loss of human life. Anger at his engineers for not catching it, at *himself* for not catching it. And a bone-deep fear at the challenges that lay ahead.

He was six months into this job. This was a massive recall. It felt blindingly unfair.

He raked a hand through his hair. "I'll fly back tonight."

"Good," said his COO. "Sorry again to intrude."

His brain was too full to move right away. He stood absorbing the brilliance of the day, the peace and serenity of the vista in front of him. It was like being transported from heaven to hell.

When he could no longer avoid reality, he turned and headed up to the cottage. Diana was in the kitchen, leaning against the counter, nursing a cup of coffee. His body absorbed the sight of her long, bare legs in the short silk robe with the greedy recall of a man who'd lost himself in all that beauty the night before and wanted to do it again.

Her gaze moved over his face. "You look stressed."

He held up his phone. "We need to fly back to New York tonight."

Her face assumed that smooth, emotionless veneer he hated so much. "What's going on?"

"Legal issues."

"What kind of legal issues?"

"A recall."

A frown creased her brow. "Oh. That's not good."

"No, it isn't." He put the phone on the counter, walked over to her and caged her in with his hands resting on the marble on both sides of her.

She lifted a wary dark gaze to his. "Do you want to talk about it?"

"There isn't much to talk about until we find out more details."

"I should get packed, then."

"I doubt we'll be able to get out before dinnertime. You can enjoy most of the day."

Then it was back to reality. Back to the pressures that had torn them apart before. With only a fragile agreement in place between them. He didn't like the thought of that at all, particularly because his wife's lithe body had gone tense just inches from his, her chin set at a protective angle, the coolness of the past week back in her eyes.

A surge of frustration rocketed through him. He did not have the capacity to deal with her withdrawal, with her descent back into herself, not with the dark problems looming before him back in New York.

"You're doing it again," he said harshly. "Shoring up those walls around yourself. I won't stand for it, Diana."

A stormy hue entered her dark eyes. "And what are you doing? Refusing to talk?"

"I told you what the problem is. I can't do anything until I know more."

"Were people hurt?"

"Five people died."

Her eyes widened. "This is what's been bothering you since that phone call."

"Yes."

"Goddammit, Coburn, you have to talk to me about this stuff. It doesn't just go one way. I can help. We can talk it through."

"We are talking."

"When I force it out of you. You've become this closed-off version of yourself. I don't know how to reach you anymore."

"What more do you want me to say when I know *nothing*?"

A flush filled her cheeks. "I want to know what this means for Grant. For you… How you are feeling about it."

He swallowed past his frustration. "It's the worst recall the company has ever faced. It could be crippling. I don't *know*."

The harsh light in her eyes softened. She set her coffee cup down and reached out to curl her fingers around his hand. "You don't try to handle things like this on your own, Coburn, you confide in someone."

The anger and frustration searing his throat made it hard to speak. He looked down at her delicate fingers curved around his. "It's knowing I can never bring those people back that's the worst. That their families have lost them forever because we made a mistake."

She shook her head. "It was an accident. No one meant to hurt anyone. The only thing you can do is do right by their families. Fix the problem."

The lump in his throat grew until it felt as if it was choking him, his guts churning like one of the very expensive engines he manufactured. He knew what it was like to have someone take away the person you loved the most when it should never have happened. Anton Markovic had done that when he had set his father up for suicide. He *would* make this right. He would shoulder responsibility for it. But right now he just wanted to bury his fear in the one thing that would make him feel better. That always had.

He studied the color that stained his wife's throat and chest where her silk robe gaped open. She always got red there when she was aroused. *He* was aroused knowing what lay beneath the silk. Her full, engorged breasts added a whole new sexy dimension to her body he couldn't stop thinking about. He wanted to see her. *Devour* her until she screamed as she had last night.

The pulse at the base of her neck throbbed. Her gaze met his as he lifted it to hers. "You are insatiable," she breathed. "I'm trying to help."

"You want to help?" He ran a finger from her throat down to the upper curve of her breast. "Take off the robe."

Her gaze tangled with his. "If you promise you'll keep talking to me."

He slipped his thumb under the silk and found the soft, raised peak of one of her beautiful breasts. "I promise. Now take it off."

Excitement flared in her beautiful eyes. She reached for the tie of her robe and pulled it open. His breath hissed from his lungs. She was perfection, her long slim limbs enhanced by the lush curves his child was giving to her. It did something indescribable to him.

He sank his hands into her waist and lifted her onto the counter, ignoring the voices in his head that told him to walk away. To avoid the temptation in front of him. Because every time he gave in to it, it consumed him more. Made him need her more. And he didn't want to need her.

The need in him won.

He bent and took one of her nipples into his mouth while his fingers plumped her luscious flesh. She tasted of lemons and sweetness and he was lost before he'd even started.

She moaned and buried her fingers in his hair as he

sucked hard on her. When her nipple was taut beneath his lips, he transferred his attention to the other peak, satisfying every bit of his craving. She arched beneath him, leaning back against the counter with a low moan.

When her other nipple was a hard pebble beneath his teeth, he straightened and studied his handiwork. The distended, engorged tips of her beautiful breasts made him so hard he had trouble focusing. But he knew his wife needed warming up before he took her, and somewhere he found a shaky sense of self-control.

He kept his eyes on hers as he worked her thighs apart and sought out the delicate button at the heart of her. Her ebony eyes went a molten chocolate brown as he rubbed her between his fingers.

"God, Coburn..."

He pressed his thumb against her in tiny, circular movements that had her eyes drooping shut as pleasure consumed her. "Look at me," he commanded, stilling his movement. She opened them, hot color claiming her cheeks. Slowly, sensuously, he worked her, watching her orgasm build in her eyes.

Satisfaction lanced through him. "That's the way I want you, sweetheart, wide-open, so I can see every part of you."

She was too far gone to respond. He moved his thumb against her harder, faster, until she threw back her head, a shudder raking through her.

He shoved his shorts off and pulled her to the edge of the counter. Her thighs were trembling as he wrapped them around him and entered her with an insistent surge that took him all the way to her core. Her moan was pure satisfaction.

The sensation of being encased in velvety, hot muscle overwhelmed his control. In less than a dozen hard strokes, he found his release, his hips jerking hard against her as he spilled himself inside her.

Her name as he uttered it on a low, urgent groan sounded like the desperate plea of a man who wanted everything he couldn't have.

CHAPTER TWELVE

GOD, SHE LOVED New York in the fall.

Diana smiled at the little terrier kicking up the red-and-orange-hued leaves on the sidewalk of their Chelsea neighborhood, sidestepped the frantic little pup and made her way toward the butcher shop. An extravaganza of color bursting with promise—that was what New York was like at this time of the year. She couldn't get enough of it.

If it was the last place she'd expected to be, and she'd given up her dream of Africa, she now knew everything happened for a reason. She and Coburn clashing that night on his balcony, conceiving their baby, had been meant to make them face their feelings. To pull them back from the brink before it was too late for them.

She pulled open the door of the butcher shop, musical chimes announcing her arrival to the handful of customers in the store. She and Coburn had been home for three weeks now, during which time she'd transplanted her life back to Manhattan, focused on supporting her husband through what might be the biggest challenge of his career with this recall and bought a new home in Chelsea.

After grudgingly agreeing to go see the insanely expensive town house Coburn's business acquaintance was selling, she'd fallen in love with the wildflower garden in the back rather than the extensive entertaining spaces and gleaming kitchen. She'd also come to love Chelsea. Coburn was right. It was the perfect place to bring up a child: vibrant, hip and family friendly, miles away from the very proper environment she'd been raised in. And maybe she needed that—to start over in every way with her husband.

She gave the butcher her order for the dinner they had planned with Frankie and Harrison and sat on a stool by the window to wait. Something had happened the night she and Coburn had come together in that raging storm that had electrified them both. She had finally penetrated the rock-hard exterior he'd adopted. Maybe not as completely as he had scaled her defenses, because her husband was now a complex enigma of a man she wasn't sure she'd ever know entirely. But she did know when he expressed true emotion.

It had ruled him in the kitchen that morning on the island when he'd confided in her about the recall and taken her with a desperate need he couldn't hide. Since then, he'd been letting her in. He was allowing her to support him through this crisis. It was clear he wanted, *needed* her on a level that was more than just sex. What that was, exactly, she wasn't sure. It was the piece still tugging at her gut.

She turned her attention to the stream of passersby, tucked into jackets and sweaters to ward off the chill. She couldn't deny it was strange to be running domestic errands instead of battling her way through a list of cases in the OR. She missed it. She missed it as if a piece of her identity had been stripped away. But she also knew this break had been good for her. She'd needed to take a step back and think about what she really wanted. Rescuing James on that cliff that night had confirmed everything about why she'd become a doctor. She needed to get back to that feeling, to that soul-deep confirmation that what she did mattered.

But right now her husband needed her. Her marriage

had to come first for the next few months until her husband weathered this crisis.

Coburn's words on the way home from the Kents that night had stayed with her. She couldn't spend her life allowing what-ifs to rule. She'd spent her entire marriage doing that. Wondering every time she and Coburn had an argument if he was going to leave. Petrified he would. She'd crippled them before they'd even gotten started. And it hadn't just been her marriage. She'd spent her life afraid to put herself out there. Afraid to say what she really wanted. Burying her identity in a job she couldn't let go of because to do that meant she had to figure out who she really was.

She was figuring that out now. This opportunity she had with Coburn to make things right, to grab the happiness she knew they could have, was about building a new foundation for her life based on what she wanted for the future. On who she wanted to be. She needed to let her heart rule, not the insecurities that had driven her her entire life.

She watched a woman walk by with her toddler son wobbling beside her in a chunky knit sweater and pants, his hand tucked in hers. A throb pulsed low in her abdomen. She wasn't messing her marriage up this time. This time she was going to be the one to offer her all. And if the thought of making herself that vulnerable made her want to throw up, so be it.

"Diana—I thought that was you."

She looked up to find Frank Moritz, her mentor and the surgeon whose pediatric fellowship she'd refused to beg for, making his way through the door of the shop. She'd been so far in her head, she hadn't even noticed him walk by.

He was as tall and dominating as ever, and there was a distinct European twist to his mouth as he bent to give her a kiss on both cheeks.

"I thought you were in Africa working. Or have I screwed up the timing?"

"No—" She hesitated. "My plans changed. I'm back in New York."

He fixed her with one of his trademark aggressive studies. "Well, that's an interesting development. I wanted you for the fellowship. Why didn't you compete?"

She swallowed. Lifted her chin. No time like the present to start speaking her mind…

"I thought my work spoke for itself. I didn't want to win a popularity contest with you, Frank. I wanted you to choose the surgeon who deserved it."

He kept up that level stare, as if deciding whether or not to take the insult. Finally he inclined his head. "You were the best. I wasn't happy with any of the applicants. It's still open if you want it."

Her heart sped up in her chest. *Oh, my God.* Then the reality of her situation kicked in. She was pregnant. Even if she told him the facts and he was okay with her taking a few weeks off to have the baby, it would be an excessively short period for her to bond with her child. Nothing as Coburn had envisioned.

She dipped her chin. "I'm not sure it's the right timing for me."

His gaze narrowed. "You know what this fellowship is worth, Diana. The window is narrow. I've got to make a decision by the end of the month. Think about it."

How could she not? It had been her dream to work with him.

She nodded. "I'll think about it."

His cool blue gaze rested on her face. "Tell that possessive husband of yours it's only a couple of years. He can have you back after that."

Or not. Coburn would lose his mind if she brought this

up. She wasn't going to say anything until she'd thought it through.

Frank glanced at his watch. "I must go. You know where to find me. I'm glad I ran into you."

She felt as if a train had hit her as his tall figure disappeared through the glass door. Fate was being very cruel. To offer her her dream at this crucial point in her marriage with a baby on the way? When she'd finally come to peace with her circumstances? What was this particular test supposed to accomplish?

Head spinning, she collected her shopping and walked home to Coburn's apartment they were still sharing until the house was ready. He got home ten minutes before Frankie and Harrison were due to arrive, dark shadows under his eyes as he dropped his briefcase to the floor.

Her heart stuttered with the same half beat it always did when he walked into a room. He had the whole distracted hot-man-in-a-suit thing perfected. And then there was the fact she knew every amazing inch beneath it…

Setting the bread she was cutting on the counter, she walked to the door, grabbed the lapels of his jacket and rose up on her toes to give him a kiss. He snaked an arm around her waist and returned the kiss with a hungry force that underscored the edginess she'd read on his face.

"Bad day?"

He nodded, releasing her to strip off his jacket. "We're announcing the recall next week. The allocation of blame, the messaging around it, it's been brutal. Everyone wants someone's head on a platter."

She took his jacket. "That can't be easy."

His eyes glittered with frustration. "I want to get out in front of this. Accept responsibility and help the victim's families. Find a solution to the problem so it doesn't become a systemic part of our processes. But the more time we waste arguing over the semantics, the longer it's taking us to attack the issues."

Her mouth curved in a wry smile. "Sounds like hospital politics. But who could want you to not take responsibility? That seems like Crisis Communications 101 to me."

"The board wants to minimize our culpability. Share the blame."

"But aren't Grant parts responsible for the brake failures?"

"We're ninety-nine percent sure they are."

"Then, doing the right thing is never the wrong thing."

"My critics think we can do both." He dug his fingers into his tie and loosened the knot. "How was *your* day?"

"Scintillating," she said drily. "I worked out, went for lunch with Beth, then shopped for dinner. The highlight was a half hour spent picking out which wine to serve with the steak."

His gaze raked her face. "Diana—"

"Stop." She cut him off softly. "I was being facetious. I'm good."

He gave her a long look. "I need to change."

"Go."

She finished prepping dinner. She wanted to tell Coburn about her chance meeting with Frank Moritz that afternoon and his earth-shattering offer so badly, it was eating a hole in her brain. But now was definitely not the time.

Frankie and Harrison arrived. Vivacious and beautiful Frankie was a perfect foil for Harrison's serious, dark demeanor. Diana had always been a little cautious around Coburn's brother in the past, finding him moody and stern. But he seemed to have loosened up since he'd met Frankie; this version of the presidential candidate one she liked very much.

If she'd been anticipating a hostile response from her brother-in-law for walking out on Coburn a year ago, she didn't get it. Harrison wasn't overly warm—warily accepting was more like it. As if he was leaving it up to her and Coburn to figure it out.

They sat down to dinner. Conversation flowed smoothly and easily as they chatted about Harrison's campaign and how the numbers were looking. It was early days yet, but he was holding up well against his competitors, leading even in some states.

It did her soul good to see the burgeoning relationship between Coburn and his brother. They were easier with each other now, genuine, with none of the tension she'd used to witness between them. What wasn't so easy for her to watch was the open adoration on Harrison's face when he looked at his five-months-pregnant wife. It was how Coburn had used to look at her. Uncaring of who witnessed it, *proud.*

It did something to the tension already clenching her stomach from her emotional seesaw of a day. Tightened her inner muscles like a vise until it was hard to force the delicious steak past it.

She escaped gratefully to the kitchen with the dishes when they were done with the main course. Coburn followed her, setting a stack on the counter. He watched as she loaded them into the dishwasher.

"Olga can do those tomorrow."

"I thought I'd get them out of the way."

He stepped closer, lifting her chin with his fingers. "What's wrong?"

"Nothing." She gave him a bright look.

"If it's the work stuff..."

"It's not the work stuff."

"Then, what *is it*?"

Her emotions spiraled, swirled through the air as they gained momentum in the emotional storm sweeping over her.

I need to know if you still love me. I need to know I'm

not about to sacrifice the opportunity of a lifetime for you for this to fail. To end up just like my mother...

She set her jaw, refusing to give in to the forces that wanted to destroy the fragile hope she'd been building. "I'm just tired. I didn't sleep well last night."

He stepped in close, bending his head to bring his mouth to her ear. "I know a good tension reliever I happen to have a specialty in."

His husky, fatigue-deepened voice wove its usual magic around her senses. She leaned back against the counter. "Sex doesn't solve everything, Coburn."

He lifted a brow. "So there is something bothering you."

"I'm tired," she reiterated, pressing a palm to his chest to move him out of the way. "I need to serve dessert."

He stepped back, his frown telling her it wasn't the end of it. Frankie paused halfway into the kitchen, her gaze darting from Coburn to her. "Sorry, was just going to get some more mineral water."

Diana retrieved the bottle from the refrigerator. Coburn rejoined Harrison at the table while Frankie helped her serve dessert. When the two men had gone off to talk Grant business in the living room over a brandy, Diana and Frankie took their tea out onto the deck.

"I seriously miss my wine." Frankie sighed, curling up in one of the lounge chairs. "I'll be happy when I can have a glass again."

"Me, too." Although she could use more than a glass right now to help her unwind.

"Are you going to go back to work until the baby comes?" Frankie asked.

She lowered herself into the chair beside her. "I was going to until this recall happened. Now I think Coburn needs me by his side. My job is an all-consuming kind of thing."

"I think it's great that you've been here for him."

Frankie shook her head. "He needs the support. I've never seen things get so ugly with the board. The pressure on him is immense."

"It's been a bit of a ride."

Frankie was quiet for a long moment. Then she turned her striking blue-gray gaze on Diana. "He's been different since you two have been back together. And by that I mean settled, grounded. Even with the insane amount of pressure he's been under, he has a peace about him he hasn't had since I came to work for him. It's you, Diana."

Her gaze slipped away from Frankie's, heat stinging the back of her eyes. It felt as if she and Coburn were rebuilding an amazing bond. Yet held up against Frankie and Harrison, who were so perfectly matched, it still felt wanting.

She'd once thought she and Coburn were the perfect missing pieces for each other. He lightened her up when she got too serious. She grounded him. Until the ways they were alike, their twin ambitions they couldn't temper, had torn them apart.

She blinked back the tears that threatened to fall. She wanted all of her husband back. Not just the parts he chose to share. So badly her heart ached with it.

Harrison and Frankie left shortly after that. Coburn went off to deal with a few emails before bed while she stowed the rest of the dishes in the kitchen, then took a hot shower.

The punishing spray helped temper her emotions. She dried off and slid a nightshirt over her head. Attempted to channel a Zen she didn't feel. But the minute Coburn walked into the room, her shoulders rose to her ears. His expression said his patience level with her was about a two out of ten. Hers was hovering right around there.

He slid his gaze over the nightshirt. "I thought we decided that was going in the garbage."

"You decided that." She walked past him, headed for

the bottle of body lotion on the dresser. He snagged an arm around her and hauled her into him. "We also decided your hot-and-cold routine was finished."

"I wasn't aware my choice of night clothing fell into that category."

He made a sound at the back of his throat. She pushed at his arm, but he sat down and hauled her onto his lap instead. "That kind of behavior is going to get you spanked."

The threat would usually have turned her on. Tonight it made her want to scratch his eyes out. She fixed her gaze on his. "Let me go, Coburn. Tonight is not the night to push me."

He raked his gaze over her face. "Why? You were in a perfectly good mood when I got home."

"I would *still* be in a good mood if you could accept the fact I just don't want your hands on me right now."

His mouth thinned. She watched the loss of control happen in his eyes before he flipped her onto her back on the bed and came down on top of her. "I would spank you," he breathed, pinning her hands above her head, "but that won't help me figure out what's going on in your head."

She fought against his hold, the tears stinging her eyes reaching a critical mass. "Goddamn you, Coburn, let me go. I'm not in the mood for this."

"Tell me what's wrong and I will."

She called him the filthiest word she could come up with. He brought his mouth down on hers and kissed her. A hard, brutal punishment meant to command. She fought him for as long as she had it in her, her knee driving up against him ineffectually, her body twisting beneath his. Then she unraveled.

Sobs rose in her throat. Her hands came up to push against his face. Coburn lifted his mouth from hers and stared down at her. Hot tears slid down her cheeks. She hated herself for it, for this show of weakness. But her defenses were long gone, annihilated by his persistent seduction that had knocked down each and every one of her barriers.

She felt stripped raw, *ravaged.*

He let go of her hands and cupped her jaw. "Tell me what's wrong."

She bit her lip. Tried to resist, but the words slid out of her mouth under his insistent gaze. "I'm scared."

"About what?"

"About us. About this baby. About what it will do to us..."

He frowned. "What do you mean 'what it will do to us'? We're doing just fine."

"And what happens when you decide you don't actually want a baby? When the stress of having a child puts more strain on our relationship than it can handle and we crumble?"

"We aren't going to crumble. And I *do* want this baby."

"No." She shook her head. "You told Arthur you didn't want to have kids. You're going to resent me for this someday. Feel trapped."

His gaze softened. "I admit it took me some time to get my head around this baby. I hadn't even remotely been in that head space with everything I've taken on. And you know my family history hasn't been the best. But to say I don't want what you and I *made* together? Impossible."

That stole her words. Her breath as she absorbed it.

He shook his head. "And as for feeling trapped? Do you think I would have chased you halfway around the world if I didn't have the feelings I have for you? I could have supported you and this baby without making a commitment to you. I *would have* if I didn't think we were right."

"That's just it." She fixed an agonized look on his face. "I don't know *how* you feel. You've accomplished your mission, Coburn. You've stripped me wide-open. Here I am, yours for the taking. Madly in love with you. In fact, I don't think I've ever stopped loving you, not for one minute. I think I went to that party hoping to see you. Hoping you still loved me."

Something shifted in his face. He was quiet for so long she could hear the sound of her heart pounding in her ears. She wanted to curl up in a ball, like an animal protecting its fleshy underside, but his body still held hers pinned down.

Finally, when she thought she could bear it not a second longer, his gaze claimed hers. "Do you know how long I've waited for you to let me in like this? It feels like a lifetime. In fact, I wasn't sure it was ever going to happen."

She brushed away the tears streaming down her face. "When you said I left to protect myself, you were right. I abandoned us. I quit on us. But I'm not going to do it this time. I am in this for the long run, Coburn. But I need to know your heart isn't closed to me. I need to know you can love me again."

His eyes darkened to a deep, midnight blue. "Why do you think I couldn't sign the divorce papers? Because I couldn't let you go. Because you *own* a part of me that no other woman ever will, Diana. What does that say to you?"

She wasn't sure. She wanted more.

He brought his mouth down to hers. "My heart is not closed to you," he murmured against her lips. "I wanted to hate you for leaving me. I tried very hard to. But I never could."

Her heart expanded in her chest, her relief at hearing him say those words making her feel as if it would burst right out of her. It was the closest to a declaration of love she was going to get right now. And it was enough.

She curved her fingers around his nape and brought his mouth down to hers. Lost herself in the perfection they created together. He let her take the lead, kissing her back, but keeping his hands off her. She fisted his T-shirt, desperate to feel his skin against hers. Desperate to have him inside her sealing this bond they had remade.

"You have too many clothes on."

"You told me not to touch you."

"I've changed my mind."

"Is that so?" He lifted himself off her. "Get rid of the nightshirt and I might consider it."

She lifted herself into a sitting position and stripped it off. His eyes were pure wickedness as he ran his gaze over her body. "Now for your punishment."

Her breath caught in her throat. "You wouldn't da—" She never got the words out because suddenly she was facedown on the bed, draped over Coburn's lap.

"Coburn—"

"Relax, wife," he growled, his palm closing over her buttock. "This type of spanking you'll like."

She did. Too much.

When he pushed her thighs apart, rid himself of his jeans and took her in a hot, hard possession that stole the breath from her lungs, she was with him every step of the way as he drove her to oblivion. To a place without shadows, only truth.

CHAPTER THIRTEEN

"JACK NIEMAN IS running ten minutes late."

Coburn scowled blackly at Frankie's announcement that the billionaire investor and ruthless corporate raider, also known as his chief nemesis, was behind schedule.

When he should have been home dressing for a charity event he was attending with his wife tonight, he was herding cats into a boardroom. Big fat cats with extensive personal fortunes amassed from their considerable brainpower, all of whom seemed to be overcommitted and unapologetic.

"Let me know when he's here," he growled.

He took the extra moments to anchor his thoughts for what would be the most important meeting of his life. He was ready for it. Determined to secure the board's approval to make the announcement on Monday acknowledging Grant's full responsibility for the massive recall and deaths associated with it, despite the potential catastrophic fallout it might have for his company.

It had spun him in circles to be sure, the brutally hard decision he was making. But the one thing going very right in his life had kept him grounded: his wife, who seemed intent on prioritizing *them* for the first time in the history of their tumultuous relationship.

To give them a chance at something extraordinary.

Diana's support over the past few weeks as he'd managed a living nightmare had been unconditional. She had been his rock in an ocean of uncertainty when he thought the sleepless nights and anguish might break him. She had not doubted him once, not even when the board had threatened rebellion and his head on a platter, always coming back to the same refrain. *Doing what's right is never wrong.*

He ran a palm over the stubble on his chin. He hadn't been ready to tell her he loved her the night she'd broken down and confessed her feelings to him, because he'd had to be sure if he ever said those words again he meant them. Had to know the bitterness he'd harbored in his heart for so long had lifted.

It had. Now he had to make *them* right. Take a page from his wife's courage and say the words he'd sworn he'd never say again.

Harrison arrived in the foyer, fresh off a plane from Iowa, where he'd been campaigning. His face was just this side of haggard as he bent and kissed his wife. It was a hard, possessive kiss that spoke to the bond they shared.

The bittersweet feeling he'd been experiencing a lot lately grabbed at his heart. His brother was a different person from the hard, jaded man he'd come to know since his father's death. Frankie had made him a better man.

He suspected his wife was doing the same for him.

Harrison dropped his briefcase by Frankie's desk and walked into his office. "You look like hell. When's the last time you slept?"

"Probably around the same time you did."

A wry smile twisted his brother's face. "You got a plan of attack?"

"Total and complete surrender," Coburn said grimly. "You'd better hope it works so you can keep glad-handing the crowds."

"It will work. The times have changed. It's no longer

enough to batten down the hatches and hope the public has a short memory. The potential repercussions of not taking full responsibility are too great a risk."

He leaned back in his chair. "Why haven't they figured that out by now, then?"

"Because it's their job to hold you accountable. Make you see things from all angles. Stand your ground. They'll come around."

"Says the man who threatened me with a mass revolt a few weeks ago."

Harrison smiled. "That was before you picked this up, stamped yourself all over it and made a bold, courageous statement that will define you going forward." He rested his dark, fathomless gaze on him. "You're doing this with a hell of a lot more guts than I would have, Coburn. It's the kind of thing that either tears a man apart or shows what he's made of. You are doing the latter."

Something shifted inside him, a part of him he hadn't allowed himself to feel for a decade. "What do you think he would have done?"

He didn't have to say whom he was referring to. Harrison knew, because his father was a ghost always hovering on the fringes, a complex icon whose brilliance had both haunted and inspired them in equal parts.

"He would have done what I would have," his brother said flatly. "He would have sought to minimize the damage to this company. And it would have been wrong. You have a perspective that's bigger than both of us, Coburn. Why do you think he struggled to understand you so much? He didn't get your humanity, your ability to see the *life* picture."

Because they had been polar opposites. A dull ache penetrated the protective armor he'd built around himself. "That was hard."

His brother's gaze softened. "It made you aspire to

greatness. It made you need to be better than the rest. It led you to the right decision today. But now you have to let it go, just like you said I needed to. Pretending you don't care isn't going to release you. Following your destiny is. Prove him *wrong*."

His fingers tightened around the armrests of the chair. He wished he didn't have to prove himself to a ghost. Wished he'd been given the same trust his brother had from the beginning. But you couldn't talk to a phantom. You had to banish it instead.

Frankie stuck her head in his office. "Nieman's here."

He nodded and stood up. He had always taken his own path. This shouldn't be any different. Except it was. This time it was personal. It was about doing what was right. It was about saving his hundred-year-old legacy.

The venue for the annual Viennese Chamber of Commerce ball was the exquisite Great Hall in Lower Manhattan, a New York City landmark considered to be an Italian neo-Renaissance masterpiece. Designed by Benjamin Wistar Morris and completed in 1921, the space featured sixty-five-foot-high ceilings, soaring marble columns, magnificent inlaid floors and murals painted by Ezra Winter.

Diana might have been enjoying herself for once, amid her and Coburn's insane social schedule, if it wasn't for her husband's volatile mood. The venue was utterly spectacular, the music from the orchestra excellent and her husband undeniably striking in his black tuxedo. Instead, she was worrying about him. He had come home from his board meeting tense and edgy, the weight of the world on his shoulders, utterly preoccupied to anything and everything around him.

She would have insisted they skip the fund-raiser if an important customer of Grant's hadn't been in attendance. Instead, she put on her most striking ankle-length gown in midnight blue and focused on being a light foil to her husband's dark, intense focus as they networked their way through predinner cocktails.

Coburn finished his conversation with the Austrian ambassador. She braced herself for yet another introduction; instead, he laced his fingers through hers and pulled her through an arch to a deserted alcove.

"Have I told you how jaw-droppingly beautiful you look tonight?"

His husky rumble sent a fission of awareness through her. "No, you haven't," she reprimanded, her lips skimming the stubble on his cheek. "You've been far too preoccupied. What happened in the meeting?"

"We're going ahead with my plan. No turning back now."

The tension in his tone made her draw back. "No second-guessing yourself. You knew this wasn't going to be easy."

"Jack Nieman said it was either the gutsiest or the most reckless strategy he'd ever witnessed."

"Gutsy," she supplied softly. "To take the untraveled path is full of peril, but it also provides the greatest rewards."

His mouth curved. "I married a philosopher."

"Who believes in you."

"Yes." He bent and pressed a hard kiss to her mouth. "Thank you."

The light glittering in his magnetic blue eyes as he drew back to look at her stole her breath. "This is what I've been fighting for our entire marriage, Diana. The bond, the *power* we create when we believe in one other." He ran the pad of his thumb across her cheek, the gentle caress sending a shiver sliding through her. "When you let me in…"

A warmth unfurled inside her, wrapping itself around her insides. He loved her. She knew he did.

Her heart sat suspended in her chest as she waited to hear the words she so desperately needed to hear.

His gaze darkened. "I have so many things I want to say to you," he murmured softly, "but this is not the place."

Her heart stuttered forward in her chest. She had to swallow past the lump in her throat to speak. "I know."

He pressed a kiss to her cheek in a silent promise and drew her into the throng of guests being directed toward the other sweeping hall for dinner. A staff member checked the list and escorted them to their table. They were to dine with Coburn's Austrian customer and his colleagues.

Coburn's fingers tightened against her back as they approached their table. "Is that Frank Moritz?"

Her gaze zeroed in on the tall, graying figure set in profile standing beside their table. Oh, God, it was. Her stomach dropped. She hadn't told Coburn about Frank's job offer. Hadn't given her mentor an answer yet, either. As if by avoiding the whole subject, clarity would come to her.

Now that seemed like a very unwise decision.

She managed to secure a seat beside Frank and his wife, Carole, at the round table for ten, Coburn on her right. She would find an opportunity to tell Frank the fellowship was an off-limits conversation.

"Six degrees of separation," she murmured when they all laughed about the connections between them all, Frank and Coburn's client seeming to go way back. Apparently Frank and the client's father had competed in luge together during Frank's youth in Switzerland.

She focused on finding an opening to talk to Frank while Coburn was engaged with his client. It never seemed to come. The conversation was intimate, moving back and forth across the table like a Ping-Pong game, keeping everyone engaged.

She started to relax when the chatter stayed rooted in topics such as politics and international business policy.

Perhaps Frank knew better than to talk personal business tonight.

Launching enthusiastically into a discussion about a film generating awards buzz, she kept the conversation flowing. Frank added his usual cutting commentary, then sat back in his chair, bringing his wineglass with him as he trained his gaze on Diana. “You still haven’t given me an answer on the fellowship. I take it that means you aren’t interested.”

Her husband went rigid beside her. A buzzing sound filled her ears. “Coburn and I haven’t had a chance to discuss it,” she said quietly. “Things have been chaotic.”

Frank pointed his wineglass at Coburn. “What do you think? Your wife is too talented to not be using her skills.”

“I think it’s not good timing,” her husband responded in a lethally quiet voice. “Considering Diana is pregnant.”

The buzzing sound in her ears flatlined. *He had not just done that.* He had not just outed her pregnancy at a table half-full of strangers.

Carole’s face lit up. “That’s so wonderful. Congratulations, you two.”

“I’m only a couple of months along,” Diana murmured. “It’s a bit soon to be talking about it.”

Frank was watching her with an assessing look. “We could make it work. A few weeks off is no problem. I’d rather have the most talented surgeon.”

Coburn put his fork and knife down on his plate. “It’s not happening, Moritz. I know how your underlings work. I will not have my wife running from the OR to the delivery room.”

I will not have... She turned to look at her husband, fury raging through her. Not even the white-hot anger sizzling in his blue eyes could stem the desire to strangle him.

The silence at the table was deafening. Diana looked at her mentor. “You’ll have to allow us some time to discuss.”

He inclined his head. "As I mentioned, I have to put a name forth by next week latest. I'm sure your husband will see this as the opportunity it is. I take on one surgeon every two years. That's it."

Coburn said nothing. Carole moved the conversation along. Diana reminded herself her husband was a barely functioning human being right now, but it was no use. She wanted to kill him.

She had contemplated turning the fellowship down because of him. Because he was more important to her than a job. But she was not and never would be a possession. She'd spent her life allowing her father to make her decisions for her. Coburn was not going to take on that mantle.

After dinner, Coburn's customer suggested liquors at the bar. Coburn declined and escorted her out of the building. She waited silently at his side while the valet retrieved the car. When the young man brought the Jaguar to a halt in front of them, Coburn held her door open, waited while she slid in, then slammed it shut behind her.

She waited until he had gotten in and put the car into gear before she spoke.

"I was thinking about turning the job down. That's why I hadn't responded to him. I knew you needed me more than I needed the job."

He pulled out of the driveway. "If you really believed that, you would have turned it down."

"It's more complicated than that, Coburn."

"It's not." He yanked the car over to the side of the road and put it in park. "Goddammit, Diana, I thought we were getting somewhere. That we were finally being honest with each other. That we had the partnership I had always dreamed of. When all along you were keeping this from me." His gaze pinned her to the seat. "When did he ask you?"

Heat singed her cheeks. "A few weeks ago. But it wasn't the right timing to bring it up."

He threw his head back against the seat. "So you said nothing. You allowed me to be *blindsided* tonight by Frank Moritz, who took great pleasure in putting me on the spot. Who made me look like a complete fool in front of a client by not knowing my wife had been offered a prestigious fellowship."

"It's *your* fault. If you weren't so crazed about my job, I would have told you and this never would have happened. As it was, I was doing everything not to set you off like a powder keg."

"So now it's *my* fault?" He turned and rested his gaze on her. "It doesn't excuse the lack of honesty."

She bit her lip, trying to be the reasonable one here. "I should have told you. But you can't unilaterally make decisions for me like that. I won't have it."

"And *I* won't have you taking that job. It will consume you, Diana. There won't be any room left for me or our baby."

It was the ultimatum that did it. "I guess that revelation in the Virgin Islands about the importance of my job was just talk. Do you have any idea how amazing this opportunity is? Frank Moritz was short-listed for a Nobel Prize. Working with him would put me on a world stage. Cement my career as a pediatric surgeon."

"I'm not saying it isn't a great opportunity. I'm insanely proud of you. I always have been. But this is not the right timing for us. It will kill what we've built."

"What will kill what we've built," she countered, "is if I continue this role I've been playing forever. I have spent the past three weeks attending every boring benefit you've asked me to, *lunching* with Jack Nieman's wife, who is a total piece of work just like him, by the way. I have played the perfect CEO's partner to the hilt. And I have done it willingly because I love you, Coburn. Because I know you need me right now. But I will not have you treat me like this, no matter how stressed you are."

His face tightened. "I'm sorry it's been such a chore supporting me."

"Take the ultimatum back," she said levelly, "and we can talk about this."

"No."

She tried to control the bitterness, the sadness that filled her at his total lack of give in this relationship. But she couldn't manage it. Not this time.

"You know what, Coburn? You don't want me. You want that mirage you were talking about. A wife intelligent enough to turn you on, but not so ambitious she might actually challenge your need for control. I hate to burst your bubble, but *she doesn't actually exist.*"

She reached for the door handle and yanked it open. Coburn curled his fingers around her arm. "What the hell are you doing?"

"Putting a halt to this before we implode." She shook off his hand and slid out of the car. "This time I *am* saving us, Coburn. Let me know when you're ready to start acting like a reasonable human being."

He got out of the car. "Goddamn you, Diana, do not walk out on me again. You do it this time and we're done."

She was too busy crossing the street to flag down a cab coming the other way.

Damn him. Just when she'd let hope take over. When she'd allowed her heart to feel everything for him, he had to prove some things never changed.

CHAPTER FOURTEEN

A SOBER GRAY suit will strike exactly the right note.

Coburn stood in front of the magnificent gold-accented steel structure that was the Grant Industries skyscraper, a tight feeling in his chest as he looked up at the building his father had built. He wasn't sure the custom-tailored, charcoal-gray suit he had worn this morning per his crisis communications expert's advice was going to be enough to convince the world that the iconic Grant brand was still to be trusted after producing the parts that had taken the lives of five people and injured countless more.

His father, who had made Grant into a symbol of the American dream, would roll over in his grave if he knew what he was about to do. His brother, one of the great business brains on the planet, would have chosen another path. The board had fought him tooth and nail to take a more conservative route. And yet through it all, his conviction about doing what was right had remained. He hoped that by acting with honor, transparency, his legacy would weather the storm he was about to unleash.

What the hell do you think you're doing?

He could almost feel the bite of his father's voice, picture the sting of his gray gaze as it lashed over him. Clifford Grant's blinding ambition had come before everything. Before his family, before his own mental well-being. And Coburn realized now he had been angry for a very long time—at his father for the way he'd treated him, for taking the coward's way out, at himself for letting it happen. But he was ready to let it go now. He was poised to forge his own path. He was not going to be the kind of man his father had been. He'd decided that a long time ago.

His steps as he pushed through the heavy glass doors and strode across the gleaming checkerboard marble floor toward the elevators were purposeful, his mind resolute. Which left his marriage as the outstanding crisis he needed to address. His asinine behavior Friday evening had done nothing but prove his wife right. She hadn't told him about the job because she'd known he'd react exactly as he had. Like the first-class jackass he was when it came to her. Because he loved her too much.

Waking up this morning without Diana for the third day in a row, faced with losing the woman who meant everything to him for the second time, he had been forced to take a good, hard look at himself. To question where his need to control her really came from. It hadn't taken him long to pinpoint the source. It stemmed from a childhood in which love had been given, then taken away. From the void inside him that needed to be the most important thing in Diana's life because *he* had never been prioritized in his closest relationships.

For him to commit to a woman had been the ultimate act of vulnerability. When Diana had walked out on him, she had confirmed everything he had ever believed about himself. That he wasn't good enough. That he wasn't deserving of love.

Her keeping that job from him had triggered all his old insecurities at the worst moment. He needed complete honesty in his marriage. But it didn't excuse his behavior. Nothing did.

He stepped onto the elevator and jabbed the button for the executive floor. He didn't want Diana to take that job.

Knew what it would do to them. But he couldn't deny what an opportunity it was for her. It was a once-in-a-lifetime offer that would lie between him and his brilliant wife forever if she turned it down, eventually driving them apart.

A fist tightened around his heart. Losing Diana wasn't an option. He *would* make this right. Somehow.

If he hadn't lost her already.

Tracey, his director of PR, was waiting to do a final briefing with him before the press conference when he arrived.

"We have a problem. The victims' families just issued a statement to hijack our news."

She handed him her smartphone. He read the statement. Felt the color drain from his face at the astronomical settlement figure the group was putting forth. It would cripple Grant.

"It's a bargaining tactic," he told Tracey.

"So we treat it as one. We have thirty minutes to craft a response."

Harrison was campaigning in California. The future of Grant lay in what he did next. He closed his eyes, took a deep breath and exhaled.

"All right, then. Let's go."

The scale of the press gathered in the briefing room when Coburn entered, flanked by his PR team, was breathtaking. Every major broadcast outlet in the country was there, each of them clamoring to turn a tragedy into prime-time news.

His rock-solid readiness of earlier that morning had been shattered by the preemptive tactics of the class action suit, leaving him raw and shaken. By attempting to do the right thing and win in the court of public opinion, he had exposed Grant to a well-orchestrated, perfectly timed opening salvo by the opposing counsel. One that could devastate it.

He scanned the room, his gaze moving over the far wall, where Jack Nieman and a couple of other board members stood. The sight of the stunning dark-haired woman standing to his right left his heart suspended in midbeat as his gaze locked with his wife's.

She had come. She had kept her promise to be there for him, despite the rash ultimatum he'd thrown at her on Friday night. The discovery made his knees go weak.

Diana's dark gaze was steady and clear as she stared at him across the sea of faces. *Stay the course*, her eyes said. *What's right is never wrong.*

It reinforced everything his wavering brain needed to hear.

Tracey touched his arm. His heart kicked back into motion as he pulled his gaze away from his wife and he and his director of PR walked to the front of the room. Tracey stepped onto the podium, introduced him and indicated he'd give a short statement followed by a Q&A. The Q&A had been his decision. Tracey had warned him it might get ugly, likely *would* get ugly, but the only thing on his mind was total and complete transparency.

He read the statement. Watched the frown on Jack Nieman's face grow as he took total responsibility for a tragedy that could have been prevented. The buzzing room went completely silent as he apologized to the families of the victims and vowed to do right by them. "It has not been Grant's finest moment," he finished, "but we will earn your trust again. I promise you that."

Tracey stepped forward and began fielding questions. The first, from a national news reporter in the front row, had him closing his eyes.

"What do you think your father would say if he was here today?"

He opened them. "He would say we need to do better. And we will."

The crucifixion went on for fifty minutes. Settlement numbers were thrown at him. Questions about the company's safety protocols. The viability of Grant was raised.

If he'd thought it was going to be tough, it had been ten times worse. He could only hope for his legacy's sake that it had been enough.

"The one-on-one with the *Wall Street Journal*," Tracey prompted.

He flicked his gaze to where his wife stood, only the space beside Jack Nieman was empty now. Diana had left.

His heart plummeted. The urge to go after her, to dump the *Wall Street Journal* in favor of keeping his wife, saving the one thing that meant everything to him, was so fierce it took all he had to keep his feet firmly rooted to the ground and nod at his director of PR he was ready.

Diana had left a door open. He would have to wait a few hours to ensure it never closed again.

CHAPTER FIFTEEN

DIANA WAS AFRAID to watch the news that evening, too terrified to see what that shark of a press corps would do to her husband following the public dismantlement of him that morning. Heart in her throat, she paced the hardwood floors of Beth's tiny living room. When her friend still wasn't home by six, she gave in and turned on the news. The recall was the top story in the broadcast.

She sat down on the sofa as the host introduced a panel of experts assembled to offer their opinion on what the recall would mean for Grant and the industry. The first question put to the panel was what they thought of her husband's performance today. Her hands twisted in her lap, her heartbeat accelerating as the tough-as-nails head of a national industry organization took the question first. The graying official shook his head ruefully. "Undoubtedly one of the gutsiest displays I've seen in my fourteen-year career. The tide could have gone either way on this one. Instead, Coburn Grant pulled the public on his side with a magnificent, rock-solid performance that was a master class in brilliant crisis communications. He may just have saved an American icon."

Gutsy. Her vision blurred, hot tears springing to her eyes. *Take that, Jack Nieman.*

A knock sounded on the front door. She snatched up a tissue, thinking Beth must have buried her keys in her purse again, and went to open the door. A glance through the peephole made her heart leap in her chest.

She took a deep breath, wiped the tears from her eyes and forced her galloping heart to slow. Then she swung the door open. Her husband stood on the doorstep still dressed in the charcoal-gray suit he'd worn to the press conference. Battle weary and disheveled, he was still the only man who could make her heart race with a single look.

His gaze scored her face. "What's wrong?"

"Other than the fact that you gave me an ultimatum on the job of a lifetime and told me we're over?"

He grimaced and ran a palm over his face, sinking his fingers into the deep lines furrowing his brow. "I was out of my mind Friday night. I spoke rashly."

Rashly. She drew in a jagged breath. "I came today because I love you, Coburn. Because I said I wouldn't be the one to walk away this time. But you have to give, too. That's how this works."

"I know." His brilliant blue eyes glittered as he focused them on her. "I was a Neanderthal. But my head is clear now. Give me a chance to make this right."

Her fingers curled tightly, her nails biting into her palms. Every nerve, every muscle, every tendon in her body craved him so badly, *missed him* so badly, she ached with it. She had waited for him to come to her all weekend, and when he hadn't it had nearly broken her heart. But she wouldn't, *couldn't* allow herself to give in to him until he proved he could meet her halfway.

"All right." She stepped back to let him in.

He shook his head. "Not here. Get your coat."

Thinking maybe it was better Beth didn't walk in on them, she retrieved her coat and purse from the front closet and followed Coburn down to the car parked on the street. The Jag purred noiselessly through the night until they reached Chelsea. When they passed the street the penthouse was on, she darted a glance at Coburn. "Aren't we going home?"

"We are." He threw her an impassive look in the dark confines of the car. "To our new home."

Her breath caught in her throat. "The town house is ready?"

"They finished the renovations on Friday."

She sunk her teeth into her lip. She wasn't sure she was emotionally ready to see her new home, not with such a big issue lying unresolved between her and Coburn. On the other hand, it was the place where they had no history together. None of their demons were present. They would *choose* their future there.

They pulled up in front of the town house. Lights blazed from the windows, casting the elegant Italian marble facade in a warm glow. Diana looked over at Coburn. "Were you here earlier?"

"Frankie was."

He escorted her into their new home, his big hand splayed against her back. An elegant, granite-floored foyer greeted them, the first impression of the character-filled historic home she had fallen instantly in love with. Coburn wrapped his fingers around hers and led her into the living room she'd insisted be done in rich dark woods to give it the warmth it needed. Her breath caught in her throat as she gazed around her. Hundreds of candles were the source of the light they'd seen from the street, glowing from every surface in the elegantly wainscoted room. Stunning bouquets of red roses filled the spaces the candles didn't, blanketing the air with a heavenly sweet smell.

Her pulse fluttered, then took off at a gallop. She turned to look at Coburn, but he was dropping her hand, shrugging off his jacket and loosening his tie. The tight look on his fatigued, dark-shadowed face threw her completely. Was he *nervous*?

He came to stand in front of her, reaching for her hands. She stepped back. “I think this conversation needs to be done without you touching me.”

His eyes flashed. A rueful expression passed over his face as he shoved his hands into his pockets. “Fair enough.” His gaze caught and held hers. “It meant everything to have you there today, Diana. I could not have done what I did without you. Every time I wanted to backtrack, to take the easier path, you were there forcing me to follow my heart.”

Her chest tightened. “*You* did it. All I did was remind you *why* you were doing it. You are so busy bristling at the comparisons everyone is making between you and Harrison, between you and your father, you don’t see what I see, Coburn. What the world sees. A man unafraid to do the right thing despite the enormous pressure on him to do the opposite. A man who has not only stopped running, but who has *surpassed* his legacy.”

She shook her head. “When I saw the numbers the lawyers were throwing around this morning, I wanted to be sick. After everything you and Harrison have done to put Grant back on its feet, how it nearly broke both of you, I couldn’t stand by and watch it happen again. Because we *are* a great team. What you said on Friday night about the power we create when we believe in each other? I believe that. I believe we can do anything if we support each other. But I feel as though I’m the only one giving, both with my career and my feelings. It’s like the pendulum has swung entirely the other way.”

He expelled a long breath and pulled his hand out of his pocket to rake it through his hair. “I was scared when you told me about the fellowship. Afraid everything we’d worked so hard for, the intimacy we’d achieved, would vanish if you took that job. Afraid of losing you… I’m *still* afraid of that. But you’ve proved to me these past few weeks that you will put us first, and I should have considered that before I reacted."

"I will *always* put us first," she said softly. "I've learned my lesson. My job was a crutch for me before. I can see that now. If I didn't let myself be vulnerable, if I always had a backup plan, you could never hurt me like my father hurt my mother. But I've finally realized you can't protect yourself against hurt. To hurt is to be human. And while it might be painful sometimes, *you* are what makes me feel alive, Coburn. It doesn't scare me to admit it anymore, because I trust in what we've built. But that doesn't mean I'm ready to give up my identity. I'm a surgeon. I need it like I need to breathe. It's who I am."

"I know." His gaze darkened. "Everything you said on Friday night was true. I have been crazed about your job. I have been completely unreasonable. It's part of what happened to me as a child. When you are continually deprived of affection, you learn not to expect it from your relationships. When I let myself fall in love with you, I went to the other extreme. I had to be the center of your world. I had to know I was the most important thing to you. And when you put your job first, it made me nuts."

"I shouldn't have done that," she conceded huskily, something piercing deep inside her as she finally explored the inside of her husband's psyche. "I made many mistakes with us, all based in fear. But I won't let that rule me again, no matter how scared I get. We are too important."

He captured her hand in his, lacing his fingers through hers, his eyes glittering with a depth of emotion that stole what remained of her composure. "I want you to take the fellowship."

She stared up at him, her heart thumping in her chest. "Are you sure?"

His mouth tilted up at one corner. "What choice do I have? My wife is a superstar."

"It won't be easy."

"No," he agreed. "It won't. But we will make it work."

Warmth infused her insides, the beginning of a happiness she knew this time she didn't have to fear. "I went to see Frank this afternoon. He's agreed to defer the fellowship for a year. That gives me time with the baby and for us to find a great nanny."

He nodded. "Okay."

The assurance written across his face that they could negotiate this, that they could negotiate anything that came their way, sent a light-headed wave of relief through her. She went up on tiptoe to kiss him, but this time he was the one to pull away, clasping her hands tight in his. "I want to start over in every way, Diana, beginning with the truth about how I feel about you."

Her breath jammed in her throat. She could do nothing but hang on tight to his hands as he looked at her, his gaze steady and sure. "When I said I was over a smart mouth and a great body that night at Tony and Annabelle's party, it was a lie I was telling myself so that maybe someday I could get over you. So that maybe someday another woman would walk into my life and I would love her with the same mindless passion I felt for you. But deep down I knew that would never happen, that I could never love another woman like I loved you.

"When you showed up at that party, I wanted to hate you. I gave myself one last night to erase you from my brain. Cathartic sex, I told myself. But all it did was make me realize how madly in love I still was with you. With the woman I was *divorcing* the next day.

"I tried to hurt you. I thought by driving you away I'd never be tempted to beg you to come back. But then I couldn't sign those divorce papers. Knowing you were walking into a war zone made me crazy. And that's when I knew I was in trouble."

Her stomach knotted. "You were such a bastard in that meeting."

"I was severely conflicted. Then I found out you had conceived our child and left without telling me. I wanted to wring your neck. I told myself coming after you was all about the baby. But part of me couldn't deny wanting to keep you. Wanting to hold on to the one thing I'd always wanted and could never have."

"When all along I loved you." Heat stung her eyes, blurring her vision.

His hands tightened around hers. "I behaved like a barbarian. I told myself I was calling the shots. But it was all about controlling my feelings for you. Refusing to allow any sign of weakness, because then you might destroy me again."

Her throat tightened. "I'm sorry. I'm sorry I left. If I could do it all over again, I would deal with my insecurities so differently."

"*You* were the one with the courage to tell me how you felt. That night you told me you loved me I wanted so badly to say it back to you. But I needed to be sure when I said it I meant it. I needed to know I could open my heart to you completely again, that all the bitterness I'd harbored toward you was gone."

"When did you know?"

"The morning of my big board meeting. I was going to tell you at the benefit, then Moritz knocked me sideways." His gaze held hers. "If there's anything we need to keep sacrosanct, it's the honesty. Even when we know it's going to be painful. It's the glue that will hold us together."

"I know," she whispered. "I promise that to you, Coburn."

Something passed between them then, a promise that this time they would do this differently. That this time *they* were inviolate.

He let go of her hands, pulled a small velvet box from his jacket pocket and flipped it open. She had to blink to take in the full brilliance of the diamond eternity band sparkling like white fire in the light of a hundred candles.

"I once said that sometimes love isn't enough," he said softly. "I was wrong. Love is everything for us, Diana. It always has been."

A lone tear slipped down her face. Coburn's fingers tightened around hers.

"Be my wife again. Without reservation, with every dip and curve that comes with it."

She stood there frozen, knees wobbling, emotion storming through her. Then she shoved her hand at him. Coburn slid the ring on her finger to sit flush against her wedding band. "Lose it down a sink," he growled, "and you pay."

She curved her fingers around his nape and brought his mouth down to hers. "I love you," she whispered against his mouth. "Too much."

He kissed her until she was utterly pliant and trembling under his hands. Then he stripped her with a deliberate, precise methodology that quickly left her naked in the candlelight. His predatory gaze softened, turned inquisitive as his fingers slid over the slight swell of her stomach. "It's not flat anymore. It's mind-boggling to think our baby is growing in there."

"You would know," she murmured, "if you were the one carrying him or her."

He dropped to his knees, curved his palms around her buttocks and replaced his hand on her stomach with his mouth. His lips moved reverentially over her smooth skin, as if treasuring every inch he discovered.

If she'd ever had any doubts as to whether he wanted this baby, he obliterated them now with his touch. "I will be a better father than mine," he said huskily against her skin. "I will *be* there for our child."

"I know that," she said softly, burying her hands in his thick, coarse hair. "I never doubted it for a second."

He nudged her legs apart then and idolized her in a very different, very carnal way. The diamonds sparkled on her hand as she twined her fingers around a chunk of his hair and moaned his name.

He took her apart with his wicked lips and tongue, as he'd always been able to do to every part of her. But this time, as he spread her out on the carpet, divested himself of his clothes and took her with a slow, sweet possession that brought tears to her eyes, there were no ghosts between them, no halves of either of them, only a full and complete union that could never be broken.

There wasn't a what-if left in her head as her husband carried her to bed and left her to extinguish the candles. Only what was to come. Their baby and a future that seemed as bright and limitless as the passion that bound them together.

* * * * *